Lois McMaster Bujold

Knot of

SHADOWS

Knot of

SHADOWS

— ✥ —

A PENRIC & DESDEMONA
NOVELLA IN THE WORLD OF
THE FIVE GODS

— ✥ —

Lois McMaster Bujold

SUBTERRANEAN PRESS 2023

First Hardcover Edition

ISBN
978-1-64524-114-0

Subterranean Press
PO Box 190106
Burton, MI 48519

subterraneanpress.com

Manufactured in the United States of America

*I*T WAS THE season of cold rains and ship-capsizing winds, when the port and city of Vilnoc drew in upon itself, and the duke of Orbas decamped to his inland winter capital. Penric savored the quiet period and its reduced interruptions upon his studies, for all that his household complained about the chill. He regularly irritated them by countering with descriptions of his boyhood winters in the distant Cantons, mountain snows drifting higher than his head, which had once prompted his wife, sniffing through a pink nose, to snap that he must have been a very underfed and undersized child.

He smiled across the breakfast table at Nikys now, but she was occupied with their infant son Wyn fussing in her lap, so the warmth was wasted. Pen applied himself instead trying to charm their three-year-old daughter Rina into eating her olives, nutritious, cheap, and abundant in this country and so presented with every meal. They were, Pen conceded, an acquired taste, and even an offered counting game with the pits could not persuade her to consume more than a couple, her face screwing up as he manfully did not laugh.

A loud and urgent knocking at the street door upon the atrium penetrated even to this back room, and their housemaid Lin paused in her serving to ask, "Shall I answer that, Learned?"

Pen overcame an impulse to pretend he wasn't home, and sighed, "Yes."

As she trotted off, he leaned back and thought, *Des? What do we have out there?*

His resident demon's bodiless senses extended, giving him that by-now-familiar doubled vision of the world: what he could see with his human eyes overlaid with her profounder perceptions; dimensions multiplied, walls transparent, souls burning like multi-colored lanterns. It no longer gave him vertigo, much.

Young man. No malice, but upset. The sense of a shrug. *Winded. The rest, I expect, he will tell us himself momentarily.*

Indeed. Following some muffled negotiation with Lin, the echoing pair of footsteps tracked Penric-ward. He didn't even bother hoping this untimely panting caller was for Nikys or her mother Idrene. The latter turned to receive a suddenly shy Rina clambering into her grandmotherly lap as the stranger followed Lin through the door.

The lad was a leggy maybe-fourteen, of the darker brick in the wide range of local skin colors, with bright brown eyes that sought Penric anxiously. More tellingly, he wore the green tabard of a dedicat of the Mother's Order. Pen, straightening, inhaled and fixed an unfelt smile on his face in return for his bobbed bow and breathless, "Learned Penric, sir?"

"You've found me," Pen said neutrally. Urgent messages from the Vilnoc hospice never presaged anything much fun, not for him.

A jerky relieved nod, and his speech tumbled on. "Master Tolga sent me to bring you. We have a very strange patient, very strange. She wants you to see him." The lad stared apprehensively at the Temple sorcerer, alarming to make demands upon, but then, his medical superior had to be equally alarming to disobey. There wasn't the least merit in Penric relieving his feelings by snipping at him.

Aye, save it for Tolga, advised Des. *She'll give you as good as she gets.*

You needn't sound as if you relish the prospect.

"So," Pen said. "What is so very strange about this particular patient?"

"That's the thing, sir. He was found yesterday floating in the harbor. Three-days-drowned corpse, everyone thought, all bloated and everything. I *saw* him. They brought him in to us to hold in our morgue till someone could be found to identify him. But before dawn, there was all this banging on the morgue door—from the *inside*—and when they opened it, he was up and stumbling around, shouting and moaning. Nobody could get any sense out of him, and he tried to fight us, so we finally had to tie him up. And Master Tolga sent me to get you, because she said this just wasn't right." He nodded heartfelt endorsement of the sentiment.

Comatose persons had been mistaken for dead by distraught kin and friends before, Pen knew, though not as often as lurid tales about premature burials would have it. But...by a physician as experienced and subtle as Tolga?

The dedicat licked his lips, and pressed, "She said not to come back without you."

Tolga knew better than to tax him for ordinary medical affairs, or even critical medical affairs. Therefore, this was not...ordinary.

Pen climbed reluctantly to his feet. "I'll get my shoes and cloak."

Nikys offered him a sympathetic but firm buck-up-dear smile as he kissed her and made his way out. Army widow—her ideas of duty, whether military or Temple, tended to be resolute. He couldn't disappoint her touching faith in him, could he now.

Besides, he was beginning to be curious.

DRIVING LOW scudding clouds before it, the wind channeling up from the harbor was gray and damp, not quite actively raining. Despite all Pen's bragging about his youth in the Cantons he was glad to pull his wool cloak, the work of Nikys's hands, tighter about himself. He followed along beside the dedicat through the Vilnoc streets, his longer legs keeping easy pace with the youth's quick, anxious stride.

The main chapterhouse and hospice of the Mother's Order lay diagonally across town from Penric's street, where the slope began to rise out of the silty river valley. The merchant's mansion bequeathed a generation ago had been readily altered to its new purpose: the old living quarters to administrative and physicians' offices, the apothecary's workroom, and dormitories and a refectory for the staff who lived in; the adjoining warehouse to patient wards, treatment rooms, a laundry, and other utilitarian needs, with a new well dug in the courtyard to supply all. The front door was kept open day and night, in honor of the Order's vows to turn no one away, though it did have porters to gate in visitors and supplicants.

It was a measure of Master Tolga's concern that she had come down to meet her courier's return in the entryway. She nodded satisfaction at the sight of his prize, Penric, who cast her and her House a polite five-fold tally of the gods: a touch to forehead, lips, navel, groin, and heart, with the extra tap of the back of his thumb to his lips in honor of, or prayer to, his own sworn god the Bastard, fifth and white. She returned the greeting with a quick palm to her navel in devotion to her goddess the Mother of Summer.

Tolga was a slight woman, aging but still straight, gray hair bound back out of the way, her long tunic and green sash augmented today with a loose coat against the chill. Ordinary at first glance, a certain intensity to her features and gaze betrayed her close-trained wits. She turned that gaze now upon her guest—guests.

Consultants, Des put in. *We should fetch a fee for this, you know.*

Shh. Let's see what we're up against, first.

"Learned Penric. Madame Desdemona," she greeted them politely—Pen had trained her to acknowledge his invisible demon, which tended to put Des into a good and more cooperative mood. "Thank you so much for coming promptly. Phylos described our problem?"

"In brief."

She nodded and motioned Pen within, adding to her dedicat, "Attend." He followed, his dutiful expression barely masking keen curiosity. Pen wondered if he was a candidate to apprentice as a future physician.

"I think it will be quickest to just show you," she said over her shoulder as she led through the main courtyard and under the archway to the former warehouse. "I have, well, more than one possible diagnosis in mind, but they all have defects. Head injury is ruled out, there was no damage to his skull or scalp or even skin. Some bizarre stroke seems possible."

"Many strokes throw up bizarre-seeming symptoms," Pen agreed.

"Yes, but *dead yesterday, alive today* isn't usually one of them." She cleared her throat. "I'd been considering an autopsy to try to determine if the cause of death was really drowning, as first seemed obvious, but I expect he would protest. He awoke, or, or whatever, quite combative, in a clumsy way." Her flattened lips concealed an unnerved tension.

Demonic possession was another rare diagnosis that rose readily to Penric's mind. He'd seen such a case some years ago in Lodi, in a patient also fished up from the sea. But unquestionably alive at the time. Pen would know at a Sighted glance if this was another.

Tolga guided him not to the morgue, but into a patient chamber allotted mostly to a dozen crippled old indigent men, some brought in to be healed, some to die. For a beggar, Pen was not entirely sure if it was a better death than in an alley or under a bridge; death was never a comfortable process, despite cots and sheets and usually overworked attendants, and it took longer here. More than one man was tied to his cot with cloths, as gently as possible, to prevent injury from falling out, and more than one was moaning about it. So his human eyes did not distinguish his target immediately. Tolga came to a halt at the end of one such cot, gesturing.

All right, this man was different, no more than middle aged, probably much better fed though it was hard to be sure with the unnatural bloating. His flesh swelled around the ties at his wrists and ankles. Really, any corpse under water long enough to look like that should be more fish-nibbled, and he wasn't. His drifting eyes fixed for a moment on Pen, and his groans became louder cries.

Des, Sight.

Even with Des's senses at full stretch, it took Pen a baffled moment to sort out what they were looking at. Not the doubled and intertwined bright colors of man and demon, no, that was instantly apparent. Only a single blurred and gray soul twisted within the man's body.

Just...not the original one.

Aye, ghost, said Des, almost as taken-aback as Pen. *A sundered one to be sure, not much eroded yet by time or it wouldn't have had the strength to effect this.*

So, possession of a sort after all—but not demonic.

You know what this must mean, don't you? Des added. It was her turn to be, unusually, unnerved. Pen shared her shock.

Lips thinning, he circled the cot to examine the man more closely. While he was at it, he dropped his Sight down in to check the lungs for signs of drowning or other material obstructions, which was going to save Tolga some fretting over an autopsy. None, though the throat was swollen from the inside, as though a lethal allergic reaction lingered. No sign of hives with it, internally or externally. An odd lack of any revealing stenches.

Have you seen this before, Des? Imprinted with ten prior human lives, four of them oath-sworn Temple sorceresses of which two had been sorceress-physicians, the depth of his demon's experience was vast.

No. Learned Aulia of Brajar was twice called out in our career together to examine suspected cases, but both proved false. None ever came in the way of Learned-and-Masters Amberein of Saone or Helvia of Liest in the course of their medical rounds, either. Learned Ruchia of Martensbridge had other duties. Des reflected. *We were taught about it five times in seminary, however. The last one, you were with us.*

Back in the great university at Rosehall, where Pen had taken his training as a Temple divine, it had been only a single afternoon's lecture, because real instances were expected to be very rare. He remembered it vividly nonetheless. *Death magic.* Or death miracle—the distinction was a matter of careful theological reasoning. Whether it was a distinction without a difference had been a matter for late-night student debate, not much aided by the beer.

Judging from the garbled noises, this dead soul in this dead body was beyond forming words. No clues to be gained from interrogation there, or Tolga would already have gathered some, bewildering as they would have been. Though really, she should have noted the lack of a heartbeat or pulse, however faint, but maybe she just couldn't believe what she wasn't seeing.

Pen straightened, and said to the hovering Tolga, "Yes. I know what this is." She huffed provisional relief, but then eyed him more narrowly. He glanced around the chamber; not every man there was too far gone to watch and listen in worry. "Let's go somewhere quiet to talk. This will take some explaining." And he wasn't, he realized glumly, going to be done at that point.

They walked back out to the courtyard, Phylos tailing. Tolga surveyed the scene. It was the busiest hour of the morning: acolytes escorting patients to be treated or bathed, dedicats hurrying in to change soiled bedding, another physician trailing a pair of apprentices into a sick chamber, lecturing as he strode, the far gate opened for a cart and men bringing in firewood, the creaking well windlass getting a noisy workout, its nearby benches filled with gossiping laundresses waiting with their buckets.

"My writing cabinet, I think. Phylos, bring us tea there." As her energetic novice ducked his head and wheeled, she added, "Bring enough for three," which made his shoulders hitch up in gratification. He scampered ahead of them back through the archway.

Penric followed Tolga up the stairs and along the second-floor gallery to the chamber she shared with three other physicians, their four writing desks shoved together in the middle, the walls lined with shelves crammed with records, codices, and scrolls. Thankfully her chamber mates were all out on duty at the moment. Pen wondered what other duties Tolga was neglecting this morning for her mystery case; no doubt her colleagues were accustomed to taking up the slack for one another. By the time she had dragged three chairs together, the breathless Phylos was back with the tea on a tray, obviously not wanting to miss a moment.

Tolga let him serve the clay beakers around as she settled back and said, "So, Learned Penric. Was I right? There is something uncanny at work here?"

"Very. And rare even for the uncanny. The first thing I should tell you, I suppose, is that your patient didn't drown. Nor did he come back to life this morning. What lies on that cot is still a corpse, animated by a sundered spirit. So not one dead man, but two."

She blinked, a faint gasp escaping her lips. Phylos bent forward in open-mouthed fascination.

"I did not know such a thing was possible, outside of midnight tales," said Tolga. Her glance at Pen seemed to reconsider his own possessed, or possessing, state.

"Most such tales are overblown and unlikely, but they do have a real root. Somewhere in or near Vilnoc, probably night before last if your man was found yesterday, someone worked a spell of death magic. Or a prayer of death magic, as it's proved in the event. Which was answered by my god." Which dropped the thorny matter squarely into Penric's lap, as the senior Temple authority for sorcery in Vilnoc. No shoving this one off on the Mother's Order, alas.

"Most commonly, it's supposed to happen when some desperate person, all other avenues of justice blocked, prays for the death of someone guilty of some deep villainy; and offers up their own life in payment for the deed. If the white god hears and agrees, He sends His dedicated death demon to snatch both souls. The evil target is supposed, or at any rate imagined, to go with the demon to the Bastard's hell, to be boiled down to chaos and utterly destroyed, not to join with any god. Which, when you think it through, is much like ordinary sundering, only faster.

"What happens to the supplicant's soul is, er, argued. It's said the funeral animals often sign that it's gone on to a god, usually but not always the Bastard. Rarely, they do sign that it's sundered. If there's any underlying pattern to that fate, it seems to be visible only to god-sight."

Penric drank tea and leaned forward; his fascinated listeners leaned too, as though they were drinking in deep secrets. Which Pen supposed they were, but they had a professional need to know only second to his own.

"So. This means a lot of complicated things. First, that there must have been another such emptied corpse made night before last. Often the supplicant's body is found with other incriminating evidence of the spell-casting, or spell-asking, so it's obvious which of the pair was which. If not, it can be hard to tell, unless the target villain's villainy was known.

"In quickly discovered cases of death magic, it's advised to burn both corpses before nightfall. To prevent just such an event as took place in your morgue last night, an opportunistic sundered spirit trying to reenter the world of matter. Which can't work out well, as the dead body continues to decay at the usual rate. The, um"—he couldn't call it a *cure*—"solution is simply to burn the body anyway, evicting the sundered ghost back to its slow, gloomy dissolution. Relatives or friends may not understand this, imagining the deceased to be still living. If ill, a stroke victim or some such as even you considered."

"What," said Tolga, aghast at the scenario, "happens then?"

"Nothing pleasant for anyone, I imagine." And was possibly going to find out firsthand. "I always thought all the hurry should end, logically, when the corpse is occupied—after that point it's too late. Making it a fight between the Temple authorities and the defending kin for a quick cremation, which has happened, seems unnecessarily impatient to me. Just wait long enough, and it will become obvious to anyone." Pen grimaced. "Not so very different a deathwatch, when you think about it, than for the dying beggars in your ward." And maybe not much more drawn-out.

"So what should we do?" said Tolga.

"At the moment…nothing, I think. Your man has not yet been identified, so there's still a chance for that, which there won't be once he's an urn of ashes."

On the other hand, Des offered slyly, *if that twitchy corpse were burned now, there'd be no one to argue with about it.* She probably wasn't serious.

Don't tempt me, Demon.

"But where did the ghost come from?" asked Phylos in worry.

Pen waved a hand. "They're around. Sundered spirits who have refused union with their gods after death don't hold their form for very long, though the more willful take longer to fade. Eventually they become drifting smudges to second sight, and then attenuate to nothing. They can't move matter, and they can't hurt you. They do tend to linger in the places where they died, so I expect this one is a former patient who passed away recently."

Likely one of the angrier ones, said Des. *That was not a cheerful ghost.*

The sundered never are.

Phylos squeaked, "The hospice is *haunted?*"

"Most old buildings harbor a few revenants, though places where many people die—fortresses, battlegrounds, and yes, hospices—tend to accumulate more."

"Did you know this, Master Tolga?" the lad, wide-eyed, asked his senior.

"I am aware, yes." Not, her tone implied, her most pressing daily concern. Normally.

"But can't anything be done about them?" Phylos turned to Penric. "Can't you, Learned?"

"They're not like an infestation of mice." Which Pen actually could eradicate. "They don't get into the pantry, or gnaw the furniture, or leave droppings, or even carry any diseases. Invisible to ordinary eyes, and harmless, if sad."

Des put in, "Do you sleep here, lad?" A bodiless demon, Pen reminded himself, couldn't *smirk,* and he firmed his lips to prevent her borrowing them for the purpose.

Phylos nodded apprehensively. "Upstairs in the dedicats' dormitory."

He might be sleeping less well tonight, opined Des, amused.

"I promise, harmless." In the face of the lad's dismayed look, Pen added, "Even that one tied to the cot in your ward was weak and easily overpowered."

"Not that easily," Phylos muttered, rubbing his arm. Tolga's eyebrows twitched agreement. After a frowning moment, the lad asked, "Why doesn't this happen to every corpse?"

For all that the question was awkward, Pen had to approve his curiosity, morbid or not. "The theologians have many theories, but only the white god knows. Something unique about the way His death demon uproots the two souls from their bodies, maybe. Meanwhile, such reoccupation is at least diagnostic that a death miracle has occurred. It doesn't happen with fake death magic."

"Fake…?" said Phylos, his nose wrinkling.

"Generally contrived by someone attempting to conceal a murder, or murders. Most such efforts are ignorant and clumsy, making them easy to spot."

Though, Pen reflected, a murderer who really understood the details, and somehow had the clout to effect immediate cremations, could avoid that... he tried not to think, *Someone like me.*

Oh, but I like how you think, pouted Des. *It's endlessly entertaining.*

Hush. This case is bound to get ugly and sad.

No doubt, love, but you need not. She added after a thoughtful moment, *You need to not to.*

Pen didn't try to answer that.

He rubbed his face, wondering what he should do next. "How are you trying to identify your corpse?" he asked Tolga.

"The fishermen and the constables who brought him in are asking around the town and harbor after missing men, and are supposed to send any who know of such over here."

Probably a faster sweep of the city than Pen could make. He might hope for some quick resolution there. "Meanwhile, please put out the word in your Order to be on the watch for any other stroke victims or other mysterious illnesses for whom healers might have been called during the last day or so. I'll stop by the main temple and ask for reports on deaths and apparent-near-deaths." Anything to narrow his search—he didn't want to end up quartering all of Vilnoc in the rain with Des's Sight cast out like a fishing net, looking for another ghost among the lurking many that had housed itself in dead meat. Such a brute-force solution, he knew from experience, would be an exhausting and frustrating ploy. Worse, the other half of this puzzle might lie outside the city walls, anywhere within a dozen miles around. Or farther. Des's magics had a limited range, but the gods encompassed the world.

What else. "Do you know where Learned Dubro is today?" One of Pen's two fellow sorcerers in Vilnoc, and a student of medicine, though he couldn't have been here or Tolga would have tapped him first.

"He went off to Izbetsia last week."

Dubro's home village. "In this weather?" The roads would be mires.

"His daughter-in-law is about to give birth to his third grandchild. I don't expect he'll be back till that's over."

"Ah." Pen smiled understanding, and concealed disappointment. No help there. He turned to Phylos. "In that case... I'd like you to run over to the Bastard's chapterhouse and ask after

Madame Alixtra, request her to come here." A belated glance at Tolga won a nod of permission for conscripting her courier. "Wait, I'll give you a note." He seized a quill and a scrap of Tolga's paper, and, after trying to imagine how to explain this, just made it a short summons. He waved the scrap to dry it, twisted into a screw, and handed it to Phylos, who seemed to accept it with the willingness of a dog offered a walk.

"Who is she, sir?"

"My, hm, student sorceress, I suppose you could say. In training, like you. She should see your patient."

"Like the physicians here taking in all the apprentices to look at the weird cases?" asked Phylos knowingly.

"Very like that." Further description foundered on Alixtra's complexities. "She's rather grave, but quite nice once you get to know her."

For a retired assassin, murmured Des, which Pen ignored.

"Off you go now."

Not averse, Phylos scampered out.

"So much energy," said Pen. Had he ever been like that? Would Wyn, someday?

Yes, said Des. Efficiently.

"Mother bless us, yes," sighed Tolga. "It does give me hope for our future."

Pen could only nod agreement.

WHILE WAITING for Alixtra, Pen had Tolga take him to the storeroom to examine the clothes their—*patient* did not seem the right term—mystery corpse had been found wearing. Such had proved useful before. But it turned out to be only a shabby linen night-shirt, without even pockets to conceal some useful clue like, say, a handkerchief embroidered with the deceased's initials. The garment was quite plain, obviously not the possession of a rich man, almost worn out enough to be the sort of castoff given to a beggar. Poverty, or just frugality?

How the man so dressed had ended up face-down in the Vilnoc harbor night before last was more of a puzzle. Fallen from the deck of an anchored ship when he arose in the night to piss over the side? Or staggered from a pier when the spell struck him, likewise? Assuming he was the target and not the supplicant.

Whichever, if he hadn't got himself into the harbor, someone must have put him there, which at least promised a potential witness or two. The supplicant might have had an accomplice designated to clean up after the spell, or prayer, trying to conceal the uncanny effort. It was harder to imagine someone doing so for the target, who would have appeared to die unexpectedly of some sudden fit.

Pen gave up trying to eke any more information from this meager cloth, and soon afterward Phylos returned, Alixtra in tow.

Pen was pleased to see the Cedonian expatriate looking well this morning, and so was her young demon Arra. Alixtra was a slender woman in her mid-twenties, with dark hair and eyes, her peninsular coppery skin alloyed with lighter islander bronze. Her sober street clothes were topped by a belted surplice of an acolyte of the Bastard's Order, its appliqué of two hands, thumb up and thumb down, marker of her calling and place. And, in this weather, an extra layer against the chill. She would have a few more years of study before it could be replaced with a divine's vestments and shoulder braid like Pen's, though the silver cord in her sash proclaimed, or warned, of her status as already a Temple sorceress.

Arra, as a new chaos elemental, had formerly possessed or been possessed of a wild weasel, but the past eight months of imprinting by her rider was humanizing her rapidly. Both his students, Pen thought, were coming along nicely, settling into peaceful Vilnoc and each other after their appallingly difficult start.

"Did Phylos explain our problem?" he asked her.

"Yes, but it wasn't easy to understand."

Pen thought that was probably polite phrasing for *incomprehensibly jumbled.*

"Best to show you first. Then what follows will make more sense."

They all trooped once more into the patient chamber, Pen, Alixtra, the curious Phylos and the concerned Tolga. Alixtra's second sight had as little problem as Pen's in discerning the inherent wrongness of this ghostly occupation, and she made a perturbed face.

"You would have no trouble identifying this if you saw another instance?" he murmured to her.

She shook her head. "None. But I see why it was hard to describe." She glanced around, made uneasy not only by their moaning corpse, but by his scarcely less disturbing fellow dying patients. Pen was unfortunately used to it, but he was still glad not to linger. They repaired again to the privacy of Tolga's writing cabinet.

As they sat, Tolga asked Pen, "Should I inform the magistrate's office of this? As a murder? Or what?"

"Ngh, maybe not yet. At least not until our subject is more obviously dead. It would just confuse them. And it's really less murder than suicide and execution. Or maybe sacrifice and execution. Successful death magic, by its nature, is beyond the purview of the city's or the duke's courts, or even the ecclesiastic inquiries of the Father's Order. It's sometimes dubbed justice when all justice fails. Handed off to a different god, as it were." Pen sighed. "Although I will certainly have to write up a full report for the archdivine, with a copy to be filed at my own chapterhouse. The authorities…well, that would be me, for this. The others can wait. For one thing, there's far too much still unknown."

Frowning, he added, "The two principals have passed from any reach of human help. My obligation is for whatever distress and confusion they've left behind among the living who knew them. And we really can't leave these corpses shambling around."

Alixtra almost smiled. "Untidy, Learned?"

"Very."

"So what do we do next?" asked Tolga.

"I thought, while you collect any news of odd illnesses that have come to your Order in the last, oh, three days, Alixtra and I can go over to the main temple and see what deaths have been reported." Which would also give him a chance to introduce Alixtra to the skills of extracting useful information from Temple scribes and their hoarded records.

"Would the other one even have been recognized as a death?" said Alixtra.

"If not possessed by another ghost, certainly."

"What are the chances of that?"

Really, Pen had no idea. *Des? "To be possessed? Likely. To be recognized as dead if so? Slim,"* she answered aloud for him. Yes, even a physician as experienced as Tolga had been intensely confused. "Though neighborhood divines might also have been roped in for a family member suddenly appearing to go mad, or whatever."

"If we get no direction from any of those casts," Pen went on, "we may end up just searching the city by Sight, for which I'd be grateful for your help, Alixtra." That would certainly speed up a tedious and wearing task.

She nodded, dark eyes somber, and rose with him to pursue this next errand.

AN HOUR spent at the Temple archives proved unfruitful. While the local divines recorded all known births and deaths in their neighborhoods, not just the ones marked by name-day and funeral ceremonies, they did not always send over such reports promptly, saving them up by the week or the month. The few lists that had come in within the past three days contained nothing in the least mysterious or inexplicable: a work accident; two very elderly persons who'd passed away several days before what Pen judged the key time, their receiving gods already signed by their funerals; two infants, which made Pen wince and Alixtra, also a parent, compress her lips in sympathy.

Next, Pen supposed, they might visit each of Vilnoc's dozen neighborhood temples in turn. Their pious stewards were more likely than most to have heard gossip about distressed households in their care. Starting with those near the harbor, and keeping Des's and Arra's senses extended while they walked, just in case.

First stop was on the southeast side near the hospice, where they had to wait for the gray-haired divine to finish a naming-day ceremony. Though fascinated and disturbed by Pen's tale, he had no leads, but he promised to send word if anything came up. Passing the Mother's Order again, Pen swung in to check if Tolga had fresher news. They found the porter in conversation with another visitor; he waved Penric down.

"Learned Penric, sir. I think this one may be for you." He nodded to the young fellow waiting, who was shifting nervously from foot to foot.

"And you would be…?" Though Pen could tell much just by looking at him. Of skinny build and average peninsular coloration, he had the hunched shoulders, nearsighted squint, and inky fingers that marked a scribe or clerk. More tellingly, he wore a gray tabard over his somewhat shabby street wear with the patch of the duke's harbor customs sewn to its breast.

The young man, taking in Pen's vestments and shoulder braid and Alixtra's surplice of the Bastard's Order, ducked his head warily. "Uh, learned sir. Acolyte, ma'am. My name's Ziah. I'm employed at the customs office down at the docks. Our supervisor

Master Therneas didn't come to work yesterday or today, and he isn't at his rooms, and we heard the rumor about the drowned man that was found, so they said I should come over here and be sure it wasn't him." He licked his lips. "Will I have to go into the morgue?" The notion plainly did not entice him.

"Not exactly. Ah." Pen looked up as Tolga arrived, obviously having been sent for by the porter's girl page who trotted at her heels. "Master Tolga. We may have some help, here."

"Oh?"

Clerk Ziah reintroduced himself and his errand, and she pursed her lips and said, "Well, come look. We can continue from that." Her measured words were medically reserved, though it was plain from the interested expressions of porter and page that gossip about their bizarre patient must be all over the chapterhouse by now.

Once again, their augmented party trailed through to the indigent men's ward. Tolga stopped at the end of the cot where their bloated...corpse was tied, jerking obsessively against his cloth bindings and moaning. She gestured. "Do you know him?"

By Ziah's dropped jaw, he did, though he ventured closer to stare. "Master Therneas...?" At the lack of return recognition or any coherent response, his ink-stained hand reached out, then cringed back. "What's wrong with him? Why is he all swollen up? Why can't he talk?"

Pen and Tolga exchanged nods, and Pen said, "Let's go outside to discuss that."

The courtyard had quieted down, no one working the well windlass right now, so Pen led to its benches. Tolga, Ziah, and Alixtra settled upon one, and Pen leaned against the well stones facing them.

Ziah turned to Tolga and asked worriedly, "So what happened to him? Can you make him better?"

"Mm, no. His prognosis is not good. Learned Penric? What do you wish to say?" Tossing the problem to him, aye. It wasn't exactly unfair—the work of the Mother's Order normally ended at death, when the deceased's body was passed back, usually, to relatives, or if there were none to the charity of the nearby temple. And it had to be Pen's decision which of his own Order's secrets to share with the unvowed.

There was already nothing secret about this within the chapterhouse, nor outside it either once its less reticent staff went home for the night to tell the gruesome tale. The facts were bad enough, but the distortions and embellishments of rumor would be worse. Emulation of the rite was naturally limited, first, by the lethal cost of the casting, and second, by the god. There was no such thing as mistaken successful death magic. Faked death magic had no such limits, unfortunately, and Pen winced at the thought of having to deal with an ensuing outbreak of would-be-clever murders.

No help for it. Pen hitched himself up to a perch on the low stone wall and began the basic lecture on death magic-or-miracle once more. Ziah's eyes grew wider and wider as he spoke. Horrified, yes; grief stricken, no, and Pen wondered if there was anything to make of in that.

"So my first question, or one of them, is, was your Master Therneas the supplicant or the recipient? And in either case, how did his body end up in the harbor? He was dressed only in his nightshirt when he was fished out." Really, if he was the target of a midnight revenge, he should more likely have been found dead in his bed the next morning. "Did he have any enemies, anyone with a known grudge against him? Or the reverse, anyone who had done him some great unrighted wrong?"

Ziah shook his head from side to side. "I have no idea, sir. I'm only a junior copyist, so far. I keep ledgers and file receipts, and do whatever other chores I'm told to." The undesirable ones, his tone suggested. Such as this errand.

"Does Therneas have family in town?"

"I don't think so. He lives alone, anyway. I believe he hailed from some village up the coast, but I'm not sure."

"Hm. Can you take me to his rooms?"

"I suppose so, sir, but we can't get in. They're locked. I didn't think he could have slept through my knocking, though."

"Not a problem," said Pen. Though it might be better to have the landlord, rather than Des, open it for him. Just in case magistrates became involved later, plus he preferred not to demonstrate the extent of his skills—less for fear of some false accusation, than of more persons wanting him to *do* things for them, disrupting his own tasks. *Like now.* "I'll need to visit your customs office as well, but let's start with his chambers." Private evidence seemed more likely to be found there.

"All right…" said Ziah doubtfully.

OUTSIDE THE hospice, Pen thought to ask Alixtra, "So what of your duties did I interrupt for this?"

"Nothing too urgent. Reading the next chapter of theology under Learned Sioann's tutelage. Dedicat Seuka is watching Kittio for me."

Widowed Alixtra's now six-year-old son, presently flourishing along with her in the Vilnoc chapterhouse of their Order. Pen nodded. "Do you need to get back?"

"Not right away. What did you have in mind for me?"

"I thought we could split up to ask around the temples. And if we get nothing from that, to divide and search the town by Sight." Which would cut the time for both prospective undertakings in half. "But it might be better to see Master Therneas's lodgings first, in case it helps narrow things down. Do you want to go along?"

"Oh, yes," said Alixtra, a muted grin flickering over her mouth. "You can't raise so many questions and then leave me dangling."

Alixtra, for all her reserve, lacked squeamishness, and Pen was glad of it, however hard the life that had given her such an iron stomach had been. "Good. On we go, then." He waved the customs clerk ahead of them.

Therneas's chambers, it turned out, were on the second floor of a neat house on a side street near the Customs building, divided among half-a-dozen other residents, mostly also unmarried men with better-paying jobs around the harbor. Ziah observed it a trifle enviously. They let themselves in through its wrought-iron front gate, unlocked in the daytime. Its courtyard, Pen judged, would be quite pleasant in better weather. They found the landlady in the ground-floor kitchen along with her scullion, cleaning up after breakfast and preparing for supper for her boarders.

Pen curtailed his explanation to *found in the harbor, lies deathly ill in the Mother's hospice*, and, after his assurances of *no, nothing contagious*, let his *Duke Jurgo's court sorcerer, detailed to investigate* overbear any doubts about letting him in. Climbing after her to the single gallery above the courtyard, Pen added, "When did you last see Master Therneas?"

"He took his dinner in his rooms night before last. He always does—it's paid-for. He went out after that, the way he does sometimes. But he never staggers back roaring drunk, or with a party of noisy friends, or after I bolt the gate, so I don't ask where. I closed up that night all the same because I thought he'd already come back and gone to bed." She frowned. "Now, when he didn't take his meals yesterday, or this morning, I thought that was strange, but the gentlemen do go off without saying sometimes, never mind the inconvenience to me, and don't care for being questioned about it. I thought of asking at his counting-house if he didn't turn up tonight, but I never imagined him *drowned*." She shook her head and *tsk'd*. Not exactly an expression of agonized grief, that.

"Thank you," he told her when she'd unlocked the door for them. "That will be all we need." A bit reluctantly, she took the broad hint and left them to it.

Therneas rented two rooms, a sitting room and adjoining bedchamber. It reminded Pen of his bachelor days spent roosting in the palaces of his assorted patrons. The place was kept neatly enough, no more clutter than might be left by a man departing for a day at work. Certainly no burned-out candles arranged in a makeshift altar on the floor, or dead bodies of sacrificed rats or crows, or, in this coastal country, seagulls, emblematic vermin of the god of all things out of season. Anyway Therneas's body should have been with them, in that case. If the ceremony had been his doing, it had not taken place here.

No correspondence littered the underused writing table, merely a couple of tradesmen's bills marked paid. Even with Des's Sight, Pen found no other papers filed away. A will would have been informative, but perhaps he kept such documents at his notary? "You know," he muttered under his breath, "even for a clerk, this man is much too tidy."

Or boring, Des suggested.

His fate in the harbor suggests not. One way or another.

Continuing to the bedchamber, Alixtra noted, "Bed's made. I don't think he can have slept in it, on his last night." And a moment later, reaching, "And his nightshirt's on this wall peg."

They put their heads together to examine it, Arra only cringing a little at the uncomfortable proximity of the far more powerful Desdemona. The garment was much nicer than the one Therneas had been found in, with the man's initials stitched small inside its neck, more laundry marker than monogram. So did the man own two, one to wear and one to wash? Pen owned four, two each for summer and winter, but he had Nikys to make them for him. No crafty wife here. Frowning, Pen replaced it on its peg.

Meanwhile, Alixtra had sensibly been checking the man's wardrobe, where she did uncover a second nightshirt, of a fine weave for summer. She turned the neck out to reveal identical laundry stitching, and Pen said, *Hm.*

If a man found dead in the harbor in his nightshirt was mysterious, a man found dead in the harbor in somebody *else's* nightshirt was utterly inexplicable.

Ooh, interrupted Desdemona. *Now* that's *interesting. Shove that bed aside and check the floorboards. I imagine they'll come up.*

"Ziah, help me move this bed." It was heavy with carved wood and thick bedding, not a poor man's cot. Some grunting later, Pen knelt on a surface oddly undusty for a wifeless abode and felt around. Just...there. The long oak board came up of a piece with the two next to it, revealing a good-sized secret pocket.

Nested in it were three small iron-bound cases, locked. Pen heaved one up and out. It was very heavy for its size, its contents barely shifting. Wherever its key might be, its lock yielded without protest to Des's smooth magic of undoing.

Pen lifted the lid. Ziah made an odd squeaking noise.

Within were packed coins from half-a-dozen realms, all denominations but mostly larger. Pen had Alixtra and Arra unlock the second and third cases for practice. They held a similar hoard, some still in what even he recognized as leather Customs bags stamped with the duke's seal. He counted the value of one stack and did an approximate multiplication.

"That's a fortune," gasped Alixtra—a life of prior poverty left her quick at valuation, and by Ziah's bugging eyes he was doing the same.

"I'd guess," Pen said, "it wasn't only the official bags that Therneas filched. I gather it's not among his supervisory duties to take the duke's taxes home to keep them safe and warm?"

Dazed, Ziah shook his head. "The imposts collected aren't supposed to leave the Customs house lockup, except when the duke's guards come to remove them to the treasury."

"Well." Pen sat back on his heels. "We'd best return all this to its rightful place." Blast it, he'd been afraid magistrates were going to get involved sooner or later, but this wasn't the crime he'd expected to complicate his life. It was always so hard to get officials to understand that his theological concerns were not the same as their legal ones, howsoever they might chance to overlap. His was the god of murderers as well as executioners. And, he was reminded, thieves. Whatever this find was proof of, it wasn't of Therneas's place in the death magic.

True, murmured Des. *Yet some circumstantial evidence seems less circumstantial than others.*

Are we done here, Des?

A quick recheck by Sight spotted nothing more than the ordinary abandoned possessions of a life cut short. *Seems so.*

Grand. And aloud, "You two can help me carry these."

Conscientiously, Pen kicked the door closed behind them and had Des lock it. For what it was worth.

IN THE early afternoon streets, the misting rain had let up, though the harbor breeze was still raw. Pen's burdened little parade soon reached the Customs building, a stone rectangle that stood apart from its neighbors just off the main piers. Its solid iron-bound wooden gate had a smaller door within it for pedestrians, containing a yet smaller panel in which the porter's face appeared at Ziah's awkward knock and halloo. Recognizing the junior scribe, the man admitted them at once, though he stared in worry at the silver cords in Pen's and Alixtra's Temple garb. Pen gave him a friendly smile in lieu of the reassuring tally sign he couldn't make due to his load.

They tramped through the small, plain courtyard to the door of a receiving office, with a long wooden counter set up in front, unmanned at present in this slow season. They heaved their heavy cases atop it with huffs of relief. Ziah rubbed his arms.

"Find me the most senior person here," Pen told him, and he nodded and dodged around the counter into a back room. Voices rose, fell, rose again in sharp surprise; he soon returned with an older man in tow, also wearing the gray tabard although tied over a thicker torso.

Pen flipped open the cases, and the man gasped, his hand going out to touch their contents. "How did you locate this?"

Pen wasn't sure if that was to his address or Ziah's, but the junior scribe answered, "He went straight to it! It was amazing!"

"Did you, now." The man's thick eyebrows met in a suspicious frown at Pen. "And just how did you know where to look?"

Pen refrained from rolling his eyes. "Do you have time to listen to an hour's lecture on the way demonic second sight works?"

Alixtra, leaning her elbow on the counter, put in helpfully, "There will be theology."

"…Not really."

"Then let's just say it was magic. I'm Learned Penric, Duke Jurgo's court sorcerer and servant of the white god's Order in Vilnoc. And this is my assistant sorceress, Acolyte Alixtra."

Alixtra cast the man a polite truncated tally sign, just the tap of the back of her thumb to her lips. She did not murmur an acerbic, *Charmed, I'm sure*, but Pen could read the effort to stifle it in her thin smile.

"And you would be…?"

At the mention of the duke, the man recovered his manners in a hurry, bobbing a belated bow. "I'm Lekousa, senior clerk here."

"So you would be, what, Master Therneas's second-in-command, as it were?"

"Yes."

"Oh, good. I was hoping to find someone who knew him better. I have a great many questions about him."

"But...this..." Lekousa gestured in consternation at the cases.

"Yes, you'll need your people to count it, and inventory it, and send someone to the magistrate's office and the palace—I believe Captain Oxato is in charge in Jurgo's absence, yes?"

Lekousa nodded, biting his lip as it dawned on him just how large and ripe a shovel-load of trouble this Temple divine was slinging to him.

"My interest is not in this apparent peculation, however and whenever it happened, but in how Therneas's body ended up in the harbor, night before last as nearly as we can tell."

"I...he is dead, then?"

Simplifying, Pen said, "Yes."

"Was he *murdered?*"

"Not exactly, no."

"What does that even mean?"

It looked as though Lekousa was going to be one of the bright ones, which, while Pen approved in general, meant he was doubtless doomed to endure a lot more questions from him. He resigned himself, saying with a wave, "Go ahead and get this started." Or he'd never net the man's undivided attention. "We'll need to sit down in private to talk."

There followed the expected flurry: more clerks, runners sent, the cases carefully carted to the back room. Poor Ziah was patted down for anything he might have pocketed, to his intense indignation. Lekousa glanced at Penric and Alixtra. Pen glanced dryly back, and Lekousa gulped and prudently did not demand either of them subject themselves to a similar search.

While this was going on, Pen murmured to Alixtra, "Do you want to go back to our chapter-house and get lunch? Check on Kittio?"

"Yes to both, but don't you need to eat, too?"

Pen's *No* tangled with Des's *Yes* in his mouth.

Alixtra muffled a smile. "Let's get through this and then both go. I know your wife has some strong opinions on your erratic meals."

"What, all you women ganging up on me?"

"Someone has to."

A sense of wordless agreement from Des. Pen tried not to feel too ridiculously warmed.

Finally, they were able to take Lekousa aside to a quiet room for, Pen was sure, mutual interrogation. And the Basics of Death Magic lecture *again*, because Ziah's excited tale to his fellow clerks had done nothing to clarify matters, though a couple of them had voiced a morbid desire to go over to the Mother's Order and view this marvel for themselves. Tolga would not be pleased at an influx of gawkers.

Lekousa evicted two scribes from their rather underlit workspace, who seemed happy to be let off their inky labors and go join the gossipers collecting around the suddenly interesting Ziah. Setting out two chairs and a stool, he politely took the latter for himself. His haunches had barely touched the wood before he blurted plaintively, "I don't understand any of this!"

Pen drew breath and recounted his morning's findings—his tale was getting more clipped with practice, though he hoped not less comprehensible. The overwhelmed expression on the senior clerk's face as he finished suggested less enlightenment than surrender.

"First—oh, so many things first." Questions thronged in Pen's brain. "Was the last time you saw Master Therneas at the end of work two days ago?"

Lekousa nodded.

The landlady had seen him later, so, no clue there. "Do you have any idea where he goes when he goes out in the evenings? Friends? Taverns? Brothels?"

"I've seen him around at harbor taverns a few times."

Pen extracted the names of them, in case Therneas had visited one later that night. "Drinking with workmates?"

"He used to. Not since he was promoted, though."

"How long has he worked here?"

"About nine years. I've been here thirteen." This last was delivered with a slightly peeved tinge.

"The Mother's Order needs to know to whom to release the body." When it finally stopped twitching. "Do you know how to find his kin?"

Lekousa shook his head. "He's got none in town, I know. He came from somewhere up-coast. Or down-coast. I don't know if his family is estranged, or all dead, but he never talked about them."

"Has he any friends close enough to take charge of his funeral arrangements?" Not Lekousa, obviously.

"None I know."

"The Customs house, then?"

Lekousa didn't look as if the suggestion delighted him. "Isn't there anyone besides us?"

"The temple near the Mother's Order buries their deceased beggars as an act of charity. But he's hardly a street beggar." And even the beggars usually had friends who came to their funerals, even if the only offering they could give was a song, or a few pitiful clipped coins. Both the divines and the gods granted them the same dignities as any other souls, all the same.

Lekousa mused, "If he'd been hanged by the duke, I suppose the magistrate's office would say what to do, but that seems behindhand for this."

Interesting that Lekousa didn't seem to have any trouble believing his late superior was guilty of the embezzlement. Given the man's posthumous disgrace, there was apparently little hope of leaning on the Customs house to take over the duty of burying their colleague.

Pen gave up this line of inquiry, though he couldn't help reflecting that if Therneas's funeral animals signed he was taken up by any god, even the Bastard, he couldn't be the target-soul, who must be signed as sundered. Which would be at least one clue. Not that both souls couldn't be so lost, in theory...though with two different inflections, as the supplicant might still refuse the gods, but the target would be refused by them.

Pen scrubbed his hands over his face in frustration. "For the god to grant the prayer of death miracle, one person must be terribly and irremediably sinned against, to the point of being willing to sacrifice their own life"—whether this was a holy or unholy offering being a matter for much seminary debate—"for justice that has no other recourse, and the other to have committed the terrible, irreparable, and unrepented sin. Theft alone doesn't qualify, or a whole lot more pickpockets, bandits, and pirates would be dropping mysteriously dead." Conquering kings and armies, too. "Can you think of anything Therneas might have either done, or had done to him, so secret and heinous?" Pen couldn't, so far; the man seemed utterly bland, a handful of nothing. Well, apart from the surprise found under his floorboards.

"N—" Lekousa began, and then didn't. He was silent for long enough that Pen had to stop holding his breath.

"Mm?" Pen encouraged.

"I just had a strange thought. Memory from seeing all those Customs bags in the cases. But it seems much too long ago. Over a year."

Pen glanced across at Alixtra, who raised her eyebrows in curiosity. "Tell us anyway."

"There was another embezzlement episode back then. With all the temptation passing through this place, it's something we always have to be on the watch for. Happens now and then despite all, and ugly when it comes out. A pickpocket has to be convicted five times to lose a hand, but a tax clerk only once. Or hanged, if the theft is large enough." Lekousa grimaced. "Sometimes small pilferage, maybe from odd or perishable confiscated goods, gets overlooked, just so's we don't have to all go through that, but it's a bad habit to let get started. Not coin, though. Very strict about coin.

"We had one fellow, young for a senior clerk, but diligent. Some folks didn't much care for being corrected by him, but he was always right, quite a shrewd hand with numbers. And it wasn't just that he was bright, though he was, but that he'd keep plugging at it till he'd found the mistake and made things add up.

"One day an anonymous accusation was laid against him, and his things were searched. Found some valuable furs, and a coin bag."

"Just one bag?" asked Alixtra. There had been a couple dozen in those cases they'd just lugged in, in addition to the loose specie.

"Yes, but it was full. Over the sum that would only cost him a hand."

"He was arrested, I take it?" said Pen.

"And wildly distraught about it. Insisted he was innocent. Which you would, naturally."

"Mm," Alixtra agreed. "So was he convicted?"

"That's the thing, he never came to trial. Hanged himself in his cell instead. Which seemed like doing the judges' job for them, and premature, but there was something about his betrothal being broken off over the scandal, so maybe that threw him into the despair, I don't know."

"Was there any question that it was suicide, and not some clever murder?" asked Alixtra. Who knew something about such matters.

"Not as I'd ever heard."

The duke's court, not the city's, would have been in charge of the case. Neither were pleasant for the accused, but Pen suspected the duke's people were less tolerant of mismanagement in their jail. It would have had to be very clever indeed…

"What was his name?" asked Alixtra.

"Soudei. Kyem Soudei. Not an Orban name—I think his family came from Trigonie, though I don't know how long ago. The thing is"—Lekousa hesitated—"we never found out who'd laid that accusation. Our old master was retiring about then, and there were three fellows being mooted to replace him—Therneas, Soudei, and me. Therneas had his merits. He'd been a ship purser when he was younger, and he was especially good at spotting how the merchants tried to hide their tax obligations. I thought it should be me, because I was senior, and said so. Maybe too loud. Though I could see how they might favor Soudei, because he was so sharp with his figures. Then Soudei was out, and suddenly it was Therneas." Lekousa scowled. "We never found out who laid that accusation—it was written, unsigned, slipped under a door—but I know some people thought it must be me. And I *knew* I hadn't, but I had no way to prove it, and I didn't know who had, so I just kept my mouth shut."

"Having new thoughts on that now?" said Pen.

"Aye...that anyone holding as many bags as were in those cases could have easily spared one. And that nobody could have slipped all that coin out of here at once—some of the date stamps on those bags are six, seven years old. A hoard so large would need years of sneaking away, a bit at a time. Maybe...nine." Lekousa's nose wrinkled. "Though I don't see how it helps you. Poor Soudei died too long ago to be that other person you're looking for."

"Mm. Did he have family here in town?"

"He lived with his mother and uncle, as I recall. Not sure where, but farther from the harbor, because he was always puffed when he was late."

"Any siblings?"

"I don't remember him mentioning any. He usually hurried straight home after work, though." He rubbed his eyes and stretched his jaw, as if trying to recenter his head. "Father's weighing-scales, and I thought one huge mess today was enough for you to bring me. This is starting to look like two, isn't it."

And if Pen didn't move before the assorted reinforcements arrived, he'd be sucked into both, probably all the rest of the day. However fascinating this embezzlement case was, it wasn't his most urgent duty. He climbed prudently to his feet, motioning Alixtra to follow.

"Thank you for your time. You've been very helpful. If Captain Oxato needs more from me, he knows where to find me."

"I...oh, both duke's men, I suppose he would. But—" Lekousa seemed torn between wanting to get back to watch over his untrusted accounting crew, and wanting to cling on to Pen as some sort of imagined bulwark against the impending higher authorities. Pen solved his dilemma by casting him a polite tally sign and leading Alixtra out.

In the street beside the Customs building, Pen paused; Alixtra paused with him.

"I think what I actually want," he said slowly, "is for you to do what you need at our chapterhouse, and then go back to the Temple archives and find out where that Soudei fellow's funeral took place last year. Which should lead to where he lived. And any other records about him or his family they may have tucked away, moldering."

"I thought his death was too long ago...?"

"Yes, but it occurs to me that his relatives may remember things he said about Therneas, different from what Lekousa knew. For a dead man, Therneas is managing to be surprisingly slippery. Also, while you're over there, anything about Therneas himself, now we have his name and neighborhood. He might also be known at one of the harbor temples—if my next cast yields nothing, that could be another place to check for gossip." And whoever at the ducal treasury he'd dealt with in the course of his now-suspect duties, but it might be better to let everyone there get over the excitement of the embezzlement first. It wasn't going to be easy to persuade them that their primary concern was not Pen's.

"And you?"

"I think I'll try those taverns Lekousa mentioned, since I'm right here in the area. Speaking of gossip. And"—he held up a hand to stem Des's complaint and hers—"I'll get something to eat while I'm there. Which will give me an excuse to repay them for their information."

"Do divines of the Bastard's Order not bribe informants?"

"I'm sure we do, if needed. But some divines have frugal wives, who disapprove of waste." Pen's grin flickered. "I'll see what we can get just for the asking, first."

Alixtra looked amused. "Where shall we meet again after?"

"I'll stop by the chapterhouse, and we can compare our findings. If any," Pen conceded.

"See he eats between the talking, Des," Alixtra told his demon. Violating his chain of command, but he wasn't going to get much pull with that argument.

"I shall," Des promised aloud. "You take care of your rider, too, Arra."

An uncertain expression; she worked her mouth, and then—yes, that was Arra peeking through—managed a reasonably well-articulated, "Yes, ma'am!" And then looked proud of herself.

A softer smile illuminated Alixtra's face, as a parent approving a child's clumsy but earnest first sentences. Penric, evoking his earlier pedagogy with an imaginary fan, bopped them gently atop the head with the edge of his hand by way of reward. "Good work. See you both in a while."

THE FIRST tavern Pen visited made a specialty of ale and dried fish wafers, which even Des did not try to make Pen consume. They compromised on a beaker of hot spiced wine while Pen talked to the tapster and the barmaid. They did know the clerical crew from the Customs house, and recognized Therneas at Pen's description, but did not recall him visiting within the last fortnight.

The second stop did better on both counts. Today's hot soup was that fish stew half the eateries in Vilnoc prided themselves upon, and in its worser versions reminded Pen of what was swept out of the fish market gutters at the end of the day, but this one had recognizable ingredients and tasty herbs in the broth. Decent bread and watered wine helped it down.

The tapster had heard of the dead man found in the harbor yesterday morning, and was shocked to learn he was their semi-regular customer, the staid Customs house supervisor. Pen didn't need to confide anything much beyond that to unleash all the reminiscence he desired, including the news that yes, Therneas had been in night before last.

No, the tapster had not noticed anything particularly unusual about him that evening. He came in by himself, as always; had two drinks, as always; and had left alone at closing time, which was a bit before midnight depending on when the last customers could be eased out.

Therneas had been normally dressed for the weather: trousers, tunic and long vest, shoes not sandals. Drab colors, nothing particularly memorable. Not in his Customs tabard, no, he only wore that when he came directly from work earlier of an evening. Certainly not in a shabby nightshirt! Though the tapster supposed a man might wear such a thing under his clothes for a spot of extra warmth, this season.

"Oh," said the tapster, turning back after collecting Pen's coin. "I suppose there was the one thing. He had a dark green cloak, good wool, if plain—I remember he complained at the beginning of winter about the price he'd paid for it. It did have a nice big bronze cloak pin he always wore with it, dolphins swimming around the circle, and the head of the pin fashioned like a fish."

Pen had the fellow fetch ink and quill and draw it, as close to life-sized as he could remember, although he was in some doubt if it had been four dolphins, suggesting Roknari islander work, or five, more common among artisans of the peninsular coasts. It didn't seem an especially unique design, but Pen tucked the sketch away in the tunic of his vestments just in case.

AS HE trudged back across town to the Bastard's chapterhouse, Pen mulled on his findings. Narrowing down the time of Therneas's death by a few hours helped only slightly. Around midnight was the traditional time for people to attempt prayers of death magic. Pen wasn't sure it mattered that much to his god, but perhaps that nadir between dusk and dawn helped supplicants to get into the right frame of mind, whatever that was.

Or maybe they were just copying garbled dramatic accounts—apart from the highest levels of his own Order, the rite wasn't something *taught*, or rather, taught about. People had to figure it out on their own, in despairing isolation, cobbling it together from whatever distorted fragments they'd heard. It did suggest that whatever Therneas had done or had done to him had occurred on the way back to his lodgings, which he'd never reached.

It still didn't explain how his body had ended up in the water, in a garment not his own. It only hinted, but did not prove, that he had struck or been struck down near the harbor, as it would have taken more than one person to transport the heavy new corpse any distance, and *why?*

His embezzled hoardings were also a puzzle, the more Pen thought about them. Whatever had he been stealing all that money for? Not gambling debts, or they'd be gone; likewise if for the support of, say, a widowed mother or other straitened kin; not luxurious living, though he'd been comfortable, just enough not to make anyone wonder how he contrived to live beyond his means. It all seemed weirdly self-disciplined for a thief. Most of the thieves Pen had met in the course of his religious duties to them had led very muddled lives. Well, all right, pirates had discipline imposed upon them by the sea if they wanted to survive their voyages, but they made up for it when they reached land.

You know, said Des thoughtfully, an entertained spectator as usual to all his ruminations, *I sometimes* believe you think much too rationally to truly understand sins like bottomless greed.

I'm greedy for many things, Pen objected. *Nikys's and the children's and my household's health, and all their needs. I must have sufficient money for that. My letters, my friends. The progress of the new sorcerers in my charge. My books and translations, and uninterrupted study.* Time. *Five gods know I'm greedy for* time.

Thus proving my thesis, said Des. *You don't understand greed for money.*

Now you're just shifting your argument.

His lips twitched in her unconceding grin.

Pen speculated, *Maybe he hoarded money the way people starved in their childhoods sometimes hoard food beyond need? That's not greed, though, exactly. That's embedded fear.*

Just so.

I mean, it was a lot of money for a man, but not so much for some large project like a bridge, or an aqueduct, or a canal, or a ship. Maybe he had an ambition to build something grand?

Did you see any evidence of a grand obsession among his things? I didn't.

Mm.

Pen's chapterhouse came into view among the tight-packed buildings without his reaching any more useful conclusions. He hoped Alixtra had found something better. He was getting tired, chilled, and footsore, and he wanted to go home, but the picture of that undiscovered second corpse shambling around loose somewhere drove him on. It wasn't the sort of relict to inspire people's trust in Pen's god. Or His servants. Like Pen.

The Order's chapterhouse in Vilnoc, second in rank in the dukedom only after the one in Dogrita, was more compound than building. Its own long wall encircled the main house, bequeathed a few generations ago by some rich patron, plus a newer annex built on for housing more divines, acolytes, dedicats, and servants; kitchens, baths, latrines all supplied with water by the city aqueducts; the laundry likewise, always overworked because what ancestral fool had imagined it a fine idea to make the emblematic color of the god of disorder *white*; a mews by the back gate for a few Temple courier horses kept close for urgent needs; and, finally, tucked in the main house as nearly an afterthought among all these practical matters, a room adapted to house an altar to its patron god. The chaos of the Bastard's orphanage was fortunately sequestered a few streets away, or this place would surely have edged over from *lively* to *madhouse.*

The porter, who knew Pen well, saluted him in at once with only a slight tinge of worry, and sent his page to find Alixtra. The ex-assassin, her baby demon still half-weasel, her son, and her son's oversized beloved dog, so abruptly transplanted and summarily plunked down in this new garden by Penric, had blended right in during the past months—the success of the scheme still made him smug. The page would doubtless be a few minutes in his search of the sprawling compound. Pen crossed the atrium and took a seat on the main stairs, leaning against the banister uprights out of the way of traffic and wriggling his long feet in their damp shoes.

Hurrying oath-sworn members and lay servants either smiled or looked at him oddly, depending on whether they knew him or not; but all exchanged brief salutes of the tap of the thumb to the lips in respect for his divine's vestments. One set of feet came to a halt on the stair above him, and Pen looked up past a long white skirt, similar vestments, and the silver chain and pendant to the white hair and amused face of the chapterhouse head. Learned Sioann was the sort of Temple administrator young Penric had dismissed as unimportant in his early focus on all things sorcerous, but life, and life with Nikys, had taught him better. *Functionary* was a very just term, because this place would surely cease functioning without people like her.

"What brings you to us today, Penric?" she inquired. "I can't tell if you are perching on our steps like a bird about to take flight again, or have collapsed partway up and will need to be removed in a barrow."

Pen grinned up at her. "A bit of both. I'm actually here to borrow Madame Alixtra again."

Her white eyebrows lifted. "Is this something that's going to come back to bite me?"

"I don't think so, though you'll get a report for the Order's archives sometime. It started out this morning with what I thought would be a simple request from Master Tolga at the Mother's Order to consult on a strange patient, but it's turned out to be a lot stranger. And definitely not simple."

By the time Pen finished summarizing his tale, thankfully a shorter version as Sioann didn't need the lecture parts, she'd given up whatever errand she'd been on and had seated herself on her step, listening with a thoughtful frown.

"I suppose the fates of the four interlocked souls in your tangle are sealed," she said when he'd brought his account up to the moment. "Beyond our help."

"So it seems. Two souls taken directly by the god's hand, two already-sundered ghosts trapped in the world and past any ability to assent. If they were the only ones involved, it would be a mere matter of tidying up, but given how complicated Therneas's affairs turned out to be, I can't even guess about the unknown other. So we'd best go look."

"Hm, yes. As ever, my House's resources are yours to draw upon in service of our god's affairs. Which this certainly seems to be."

"Thank you." He inclined his head in sincere respect. It had sounded like a dismissal, but she did not arise at once—perhaps her feet hurt, too.

She leaned back instead, her lips quirking up, her voice lightening. "So—how's the book coming, Pen? Should I ask?"

"*Gnagh*," he grumbled, in heartfelt unintelligibility. "No more progress today, that's certain. I would put the finished metal plates, which are most of them, into the hands of the duke's printer, but he refuses to take any till I can deliver them all." The second of the two volumes on sorcery Pen was translating into the Cedonian language, and to an increasing extent rewriting, was giving him fits of frustration.

The first volume had been Learned Ruchia of Martensbridge's slim work on the fundamentals of sorcery, thankfully completed, though if there was ever another edition Pen might add... *No, not now.* The second, and his obsession for the past several years, was the much thicker and more specialized tome on applications of sorcery to medicine. "It's this codicil chapter, which has turned into two chapters. I can't finish it till I get a chance to ride to Dogrita and consult with Learned Master Ravana on my scheme for using magically induced narcolepsy on surgery patients. I have to be certain I can teach it correctly to other sorcerer-physicians. It's a pointless skill if I'm the only one who can deploy it, since there's only one of me, but there's a world of hurt that needs it."

Sioann, who had heard this rant before, merely nodded in sympathy. "I hope you can get back to it soon. Your first volume was a source of enlightenment to me, and I thought I'd already been taught all a divine of the Temple should know about our sorcerers."

"There's no such thing as *all*. Besides knowledge lost or, or mislaid, there's always the chance of something new." Pen brightened. "So I need never run out, or come to an end."

"I know some students who would consider that thought a horror," said Sioann, amused.

"Sluggards," scoffed Pen, not quite fairly in light of the boy he'd once been, evading his studies in the Greenwell Lady-school. Although even then, it hadn't been because he hadn't wanted to *learn*— just that he hadn't wanted to learn what had been set on the plate in front of him that day. The power to select his own plates had changed everything. "Ah…" New footsteps scuffed down the stairs to a stop by them; the breathless page and Alixtra at last.

Sioann smiled and climbed to her feet to exchange respects with Alixtra; acolyte to divine, chapter head to her promising newest member. "I'll leave you to it, then," she said to Pen. "But do report back to me when you know more, hm?"

"Of course." Pen tapped his lips in salute and promise, and she turned to continue up the stairs.

Alixtra leaned on the opposite railing and inquired, "So what did you learn at your taverns?"

"A little. I found the one Therneas had visited the night he died, and the time for when he was last seen—late, toward midnight—plus a description of the clothing he'd been wearing, needless to say not what he was found in. What luck did you have at the archives?"

"Not a thing on Therneas. Though since he wasn't born in Vilnoc you wouldn't expect a birth record, nor anything else from before he came here. He was never listed as a naming-day witness for anyone, or as patron for a funeral. The archivist did suggest we might check with whatever neighborhood temple he used—there ought to be, if nothing else, several years of records kept there of his quarter-day offerings."

"That could be an interesting trail," Pen said.

"If he ever went to a temple, or made his offerings," put in Des aloud. "Want to make a side-bet on that?"

"That would be an interesting blank," Pen conceded. "How about that poor hanged clerk?"

"More there. We did find the record of his funeral, fourteen months ago at the neighborhood temple on

Olive Street. His uncle and his mother were noted as attending, but no one else—whether not present or not named I can't say, but the officiating divine still serves there, so at least there's someone to ask. She ought to know where the family lives, as well."

"Aha."

"Soudei's soul was signed as taken up by the Bastard."

"That…could mean many ambiguous things."

"Here's another one for you, then. Soudei also had his naming-day recorded—twenty-eight years ago, in another neighborhood, but he was born in Vilnoc. Mother noted, father not. Some village in Trigonie was listed as her birthplace—she was about nineteen. Uncle named godparent and only witness, though he seems to have been barely more than a boy himself at the time."

As godparents were often appointed guardians of the child in the case of parental death with no other kin, usually adults fit to undertake those responsibilities were chosen. "Grandparents?"

"Not listed."

Dead? Estranged back in Trigonie? An unmarried young woman pregnant with a paternally rejected child could suffer such family failures.

Never mind the offense to at least three gods by the man's default: the Father of Winter, the Mother of Summer, and the god of the child, in this case the Son of Autumn, patron of boys. Pen wondered if the Son ever felt a conflict of interest; but no, the fellow would have been moved to the Father's court at that point, will or nil.

Feckless young men can easily imagine not meeting the gods in person any time soon, Des observed.

I was never that feckless, Pen asserted, then rethought the claim. *Or I was just lucky.*

Now, that one I'd believe, said Des, amused.

Or, who knew, the swain might have died, in any number of ways, before he could marry his sweetheart. The father of Nikys's older half-brother Ikos was just such a sad example.

"I suppose there's no point in wasting time speculating when we can just go ask," said Pen. He glanced up at the gray light more seeping than falling through the atrium aperture. They were just past the holy day of Father's Midwinter, halfway between solstice and equinox; still snowy in the mountainous Cantons, on the verge of returning warmth here by the sea. Days were lengthening, just not fast enough. "Now? Are you up for yet another tramp across town?"

Alixtra followed his glance, and his thought. "Yes, but I suppose we'd better borrow a lantern from the porter for the return trip."

"Good notion."

They did so. And, the landlady's bitter complaint about her inconveniencing boarders fresh in his mind, Pen begged quill and paper from the porter's station to dash off a note to Nikys. He wished he could stop by in person, but his house was not on the way— Olive Street lay on the southwest side of town, near the old walls.

He scribbled out, *My consult for Tolga has turned out much more complicated than I anticipated. I'll tell you all about it when I get back, but I don't know when. Don't wait supper for me. If I miss Rina's bedtime, give her an extra kiss and tell her I sent it. Wyn as well. I trust I won't miss ours, and can kiss you myself.*

He put a definite period at the end of that. Then added with reluctance, *Probably.*

Your loving sorcerer, Penric.

And me, Des prompted.

And Desdemona, Pen dutifully added.

He ruthlessly left the porter to draft some chapterhouse youth to carry it, and departed with Alixtra once more. With, yes, his second sight fully extended, like walking through a cloud of syrup-of-poppy hallucinations. He swore he was going to fall off a bridge someday, doing this.

Only one bridge between here and Olive Street, Des assured him. Chirpily.

Which, in the event, he didn't totter off of, but neither did he discover any but the usual sparse, faded, drifting collection of city ghosts in payment for the strain. It would be suitably ironic if, in the effort to avoid quartering Vilnoc street by street to find their quarry, he ended up doing so anyway.

Olive Street was marginally less crooked and narrow than its surrounding streets, alleys...passages. The dwellings on this southwest side were much cut-up by time and their residents, many to overcrowded chambers for, if not poor, working men and women and their families. Only the weather made it seem so dreary today. In the summer it would be livelier.

Its serving temple was stone-built in the Cedonian style, a six-sided, domed sanctuary, fire plinth in the center with an oculus to let smoke out and light in, one face devoted to the entryway, the rest to altars for each of the five gods. One leaf of the double wooden door was still propped open for the day, that supplicants might pass in and out to pray. The place was swept, the fire fed, though the frescoes on the walls were peeling with age, and the altar settings were of brass and clay, not silver or gold. The offering boxes by each altar were firmly locked. Altar cloths were newer, embroidered earnestly by neighborhood women—such as the pair of volunteers who were finishing cleaning, and who directed Pen and Alixtra on through to the more utilitarian back quarters where, they assured Pen, Learned Retaka might be found in her study. The usual stares that Pen's foreign looks collected followed them out.

The backside was the expected rectangle with second-floor gallery surrounding a space barely large enough to be dubbed a courtyard. The sheds for the sacred funeral animals would be off an outside wall. A quick check by Sight, and Pen knocked at the correct door under the gallery, evoking a "Come!" in a woman's voice.

The room and the writing table were warmed by lamplight against the fading afternoon gray from the latticed window. The divine bending over her paper was a short, sturdily built, round-faced woman, brown hair bound neatly up, seeming about

Alixtra's age; so, likely launched from Orbas's sole seminary at Dogrita not long ago. She sat huddled into her everyday five-colored robe, which looked more tossed on over her dress against the chill than donned for some ceremony. Ending the sentence she had been writing, she set aside her quill and looked up, whatever she'd been about to say converting to a surprised, "Oh."

"Learned Retaka? My name is Penric, and this is Acolyte Alixtra." Their Temple affiliation and ranks were advertised by their garb, and did not need repeating here, but Pen could see her eyes widening a little as she spotted the silver in their braids and sashes. "Apologies for interrupting your task—"

She made a *no matter* gesture.

"—but we're on an inquiry for our Order we hoped you could aid."

"Of course." Rising, she pushed aside her paper—weekly report to the central archives, Pen could recognize even upside down—and there followed the brief social flurry of fetching over chairs for the visitors, inviting them to sit, politely offering refreshments as politely refused, and reseating herself, curiosity in her face. "What can I help you with?"

Which end of this tangle to pull first...

"Specifically, we're seeking the surviving family of a fellow from this neighborhood whom you buried a year or so ago. His death was unusual as well as unhappy, so perhaps you'd remember more about him. Kyem Soudei—he'd worked as a senior clerk at the harbor Customs, been accused of theft, and had hanged himself in his jail cell before he came to trial."

"Oh!" she said. "Yes, I do remember that one. I'd only served here about six months at the time, so I didn't know many of my flock very well yet. I'm afraid I'd barely noticed him before the tragedy— he hadn't come to me for any problems. After his arrest, his mother and his uncle came in nearly every day to pray for him. Prone in deepest supplication."

Her lips compressed at the melancholy memory; Pen gestured encouragement for her to go on.

"After the funeral...well. Very grief-stricken and angry, understandably, and my attempts to offer counsel were not well received. I did try, even going to their home twice, but they didn't let me in. With all the other calls on my care, I finally left it for time to heal. They've rather slipped from my mind, since. It's well to be reminded." Her hand twitched as if wanting to make a note among her scattered papers.

"Do they still live in the same place?"

"As far as I know."

"Hm. Grief-stricken, yes, but was the anger aimed anywhere in particular?"

"At the Customs house, before; at the gods, after."

"For not saving him somehow?"

"Yes, though I did try to explain the gods' limitations in the world of matter. His family weren't much interested in the fine points of theology by that stage. Also...they seemed to feel his soul had been taken up by the wrong god. As an unmarried and childless man, it should have been the Son of Autumn, but he also bore allegiance to the Father of Winter in honor of his craft of mathematics. If he'd been signed by the Father, it might have stood as a testimony to his innocence. As it was the Bastard, it seemed more the reverse." A nod of apology in the direction of her visitors' whites.

"Was there any ambiguity among your funeral animals, that day?"

Retaka shook her head. "None I could discern. I'd spent six months as a temple assistant in Dogrita before I was assigned to Vilnoc, then six months here, and I'd conducted the rite a double-dozen times by then. Our Bastard's white seagull attached itself at once to poor Soudei's shroud, and our Father's black tomcat and Son's chestnut dog showed no interest. All the holy creatures have been at their duties with this temple for longer than I have, frankly. I've never had reason to think them or their grooms unreliable."

Pen hmm'd in concession. "For whatever reason my god took up Soudei's soul, new evidence in support of his innocence of the theft has just come to light. Another man at the Customs house, Master Therneas, was found to be in possession of a large hoard of stolen coin. The fact that he was in competition with Soudei at the time for a promotion seems suggestive."

"Oh…" Retaka's hand went to her lips in dismay. "Has he confessed?"

"Not exactly… Although for a sign from my god without any ambiguity whatsoever, we may have just had one. Hence my involvement." Pen drew breath and embarked, yet again, on a description of his day's doings. Retaka's eyes grew rounder and rounder as he spoke.

"Just as a, well, not a side question," Pen went on, "but as long as we're here, have you had reports of any of your flock stricken with a sudden apparent stroke in the last two days? Or any other impairment mimicking such a thing?"

"No… A lot of seasonal illnesses, and there's an old man in Hook Alley with a bad case of lung fever who may not survive, but that's been going on for a week. Most everyone's attention, including mine, has been taken up with the matter of a missing boy."

Both Penric and Alixtra flinched at this.

Wait to be asked, said Des tartly as Pen almost opened his mouth. *We know what happens to you when you try to take on too much at once.* Pen subsided. Temporarily. Maybe later he or Alixtra could—

"He seems too young to be a runaway, only four," Retaka continued, "but I finally tried to ease his parents' distress yesterday with a sort of mock funeral. Which is not exactly anything I was taught to do in seminary, but they were so desperate."

"How?" asked Penric, professionally interested.

"His family gathered up all of his valued toys and possessions—sadly few, this is not a rich neighborhood—we wrapped them in a shroud, and showed them to the holy animals. Without a body, it wasn't so very different from rites done for people lost at sea, which commonly works. I thought it was worth the test."

"Clever notion," agreed Penric in sincere approval, which seemed to hearten Retaka. "So what did you find?"

"No signs given at all."

"This was good, right?"

"Good, as it says little Agno must still be alive, truly what we'd most hoped for, but bad, because at almost two weeks, it suggests he must have been stolen away somehow. So I think I only substituted one sort of frantic for another. Our other prayers have not been answered." She sighed in frustration. "I did suggest to his mother he might have just got lost and been taken in by some kind person who couldn't figure out how to bring him home, as children that age often aren't very coherent about such things, but we both knew it was a faint hope."

"I pray it may prove so," said Alixtra, and signed herself. Retaka nodded, round face pinched.

So that they wouldn't arrive at the unhappy Soudei household not only as uninvited strangers, but after dark, Pen reluctantly cut the interesting conversation with the neighborhood divine short. They collected the convoluted directions to where the family lived, and made their way back out to Olive Street.

As they paced along, Alixtra asked, "What makes you so sure our second corpse will be found occupied by another ghost? And how in the world can it be identified if it hasn't been?"

Pen gestured at the dwellings shouldering the alley down which they next turned. "It's the size of the city. If this incident had taken place out in some unpeopled wasteland, there wouldn't be any revenants around, and the corpse would just rot like any other. But in Vilnoc, enough sundered accumulate that we're spoiled for choice." Did the sundered ever squabble or fight for such a prize possession, like vultures flocking around a carcass? But no, the more faded would be too dispirited to even try. Only fresher or especially willful ghosts were candidates for the uncanny tenancy.

Alixtra nodded. "I've also been wondering about Soudei's suicide. Does Orbas seize the family property of those convicted of high crimes the way Cedonia does? And does tax theft qualify as a treasonous crime? Because I've heard of men suiciding before trial to prevent such a loss to their heirs."

"I…hm. As a former Cedonian province Orbas does share a lot of legal traditions with its parent empire, but I'm not sure about that one. Though it doesn't sound as if the Soudei family had much property to take."

"That threat is just as terrifying if one has little as if one has much. Maybe more so." She spoke with the certainty of experience, and Pen waved a conceding hand. "Even if they only rent their rooms, a bad scandal could get them evicted all the same."

Learned Retaka had recalled the brother Otzos as working down at the harbor as a rope-maker and sailmaker, and his elder sister Vissa as a sometime-scribe for neighborhood merchants, and a spinner the rest of the time. Not quite hand-to-mouth, but no better than week-to-week. "Young Kyem's job must have been the best employment to ever happen to the clan, before his disaster," Pen agreed. The hope of their future, shattered. Pen wondered if his mother had first taught him to read and cipher.

Another turn brought them to the blank wooden street door of the house they sought, closed but not yet locked for the night. Pen eased it open to reveal a dim passage into another courtyard. Like

Therneas's building, it had once been the property of a single family, now cut up into sets of chambers two above and two below, kitchen and courtyard communally shared. Voices and clatter issued from the kitchen, though the courtyard was unpeopled in the chill damp. The Soudei family lived above and to the left, Retaka had said, so Pen and Alixtra climbed the stairs in that direction.

Raising his hand to tap at what seemed the central-most door along the gallery, Pen automatically spread out his Sight to find whether anyone was actually home. And froze.

"Alixtra. Check your Sight."

She gave him a curious glance; then her expression turned inward as she called upon her demon. "Oh. Dear."

Oh dear gods. The doubled vision was perfectly clear and distinctive: one live person, moving about, one distressed gray ghost, one corpse. Also moving about. Pen swallowed and continued his knocking.

Muffled grumbling; footsteps tapped across wooden floorboards. Penric shifted back as the door was thrust open.

A man's fierce tired face was illuminated by the shadowless light from the courtyard. "Yes, *what?*"

His scowl shifted from anger to confused mistrust as he took in his visitors' pale vestments. "Who are you?"

"Are you Otzos Soudei?" Pen inquired. Hardly a guess. The fellow looked to be in his early forties, the sturdy hand gripping the door edge chapped and work-roughened. Brown eyes, thinning brown hair not yet grayed tied back in a hank, skin the common paler tan of the coast easterly, Trigonie or Adria. A workman's tunic and trousers, loose coat, indoor slippers on his feet. He didn't sport a beard, but his stubbled face had not been shaved today. Nor yesterday. Eyes reddened, but no stink of drink—lack of sleep, maybe.

"I'm Learned Penric, and this is Acolyte Alixtra." A polite knee-dip from her, with a touch of the back of her thumb to her lips, evoked a reluctant polite nod in return from their unwilling host. "We're investigating something for Master Tolga of the Mother's Order." The matter had widened from this morning, but it seemed better to start simply.

"We can't pay a physician's fee," Otzos said roughly, and made to shut the door, blocked by Pen's foot.

"I'm not a—" Pen began, interrupted by Des's silent scoff of, *Don't. I'm not sure even you believe it, and it could be useful here.*

Pen began again, "I assure you this visit is gratis. Free. I believe your elder sister Vissa fell suddenly ill night before last?"

"Nothing sudden about it. She's been low ever since her son Kyem died. But it's true she's took a turn for the worse." His brow wrinkled in suspicion and puzzlement. "How did you hear about it?"

"Indirectly, from Learned Retaka of your Olive Street temple."

"That useless woman!"

There'd be time for that side-argument later; Pen declined to be diverted now. "Howsoever, we do need to examine your sister."

Otzos's gaze went to Alixtra—a reassuringly female person at whom to shove another woman's problems?—and the stubbornness of his lip relaxed a trifle. "I suppose it can't hurt," he said, and grudgingly gave way.

Pen and Alixtra followed him into a modest chamber, cluttered sitting-dining-all-tasks room, a rumpled sleeping cot shoved into one corner, poorly lit by a latticed window and little better by a smoky oil lamp. He could feel Alixtra, too, calling up her dark-sight that would lay every shadow bare.

An upset, slurred whimper came from the inner doorway to the adjoining chamber. "Want t' go *home*."

A woman…*ngh*, a woman's corpse stood hunched in the aperture, fingering the doorjamb. She was dressed in a nightgown and loose indoor coat, a winter sleeping cap askew and falling half-off, catching in tangled brown hair a shade lighter than her brother's. Her gaze jerked around, and she rocked from foot to foot.

Vissa Soudei.

Well. Formerly. What was in that body now…

Otzos went to her and captured her wandering hands, preventing them from scratching at her some-what puffy face—swollen wrists and ankles, too, betrayed her body's unnatural state. In a beleaguered voice that hinted this same conversation had been going on for a while, he said, "You *are* home, Vissa. We're all home here. Unless you mean our old village, and you've never wanted to go back there before."

"Want t' go *home*."

He vented a frustrated sigh, looking around in embarrassment. "I'm sorry. She's been like this for two days. It was never this bad before. Low, and sad, but not *mad*. She's not mad, really." Delivered with determination, as if saying it so would make it so, force others to agree.

"No, she's not," said Penric, which earned him a surprised look from Otzos. *She's also not Vissa* was probably too blunt a follow-up, likewise several other declarations that Pen suppressed on lips such as, *I'm afraid she's dead.* So…who *had* taken up residence in there? This was going to be vastly more awkward than for the unidentified and friendless Therneas.

Otzos led her, stumbling, to one of the pair of wooden chairs at the small all-tasks table, and pushed and prodded her to sit. Taking a moment to right her cap, he pulled it firmly down around her ears; she pawed at it in a peeved fashion. He straightened and looked beseechingly at his visitors, obviously with no idea what they could do, as obviously wanting them to get on with it.

Penric hunkered down on his heels before the chair, Alixtra advancing to his shoulder.

"What are we looking at, Learned?" she asked quietly. Or Looking at, technically, her Sight extended like his. "It's like the fellow this morning, only…not quite."

"Indeed not quite. Can you guess why?"

Her lips moved, compressed. Chose caution: "Have you seen something like this before?"

"In a way."

"Hm…" A worried glance at the worried brother.

Otzos's hands twitched toward his sister, then drew back and clutched each other in a new anxiety. "Is it some contagion?"

"No. Nothing you could catch by tending to her." Pen rose to his feet. "May we look around for a moment first? I'll have more to say shortly."

"I suppose…"

Pen jerked his head, and Alixtra followed him into the other room. Clearly Vissa's side of things: another rumpled cot shoved against a wall, chests, baskets of assorted possessions, but also a spinning wheel by the window, wool abandoned in progress festooning it in sad loops. Pen closed the door quietly but firmly behind them, and stepped across the constricted space for a closer look.

None of the usual ornaments of the rite lay scattered—no many-colored slagged candles stuck about, no scuffed diagrams painted in blood on the floorboards, no sacrificed animal corpses. Not even traces of such a rite having been cleaned up.

No, wait…a fragment of white wax was stuck to the boards, hardly more than might have spilled from a bedtime candle. Yet it was fine beeswax, not the cheaper tallow or oil that a sniff of the room suggested was the more usual lighting here.

Another faint distinctive reek, familiar from kitchen pantries in all realms, also laced the air.

Alixtra sniffed it too, and followed her wrinkling nose and Sight around behind a chest, which she shoved away from the wall. She bent down and came up with the swollen and stiff, but thankfully not yet liquified, corpse of a white mouse, holding it gingerly by its purpling pink tail.

Not a house mouse, free for the capture with a little ingenuity and a bucket. This was the breed sold in the marketplaces on the Bastard's Day in midsummer as poorly thought-out pets for children, no doubt to introduce them early to weeping tragedy. This one had not died of any of the fates such short-lived creatures might meet in inexperienced little hands, but of a sharply twisted neck.

One tiny white candle, no larger than those set to light a festive cake. One small mouse, though the best that could be found. One broken heart, offering up its last shreds of hope. Pen thought he'd just discovered the answer to a long-ago seminary debate over what of the many recorded and often grotesque elaborations for this prayer were essential and what were not.

So little, in the uttermost end. And he suspected even the candle was optional.

He scratched at the wax residue with a fingernail, sighed, and stood.

Alixtra grimaced at the dead mouse swinging from her pinched fingers. "I take it we've found our supplicant. The answers to many questions lay themselves out, not too surprisingly by now. So what was it about that occupying ghost that turned you so grave?"

"It's not sundered."

She blinked, startled.

"Yet," Pen added in growing concern. "I'm not sure how much time we have left before it is, however."

"It's possible for an *un*sundered spirit to possess a corpse like that?"

"It's, hm, not uncommon for a spirit to be briefly lost between its death and the gods—not denying Them, nor denied, just unable to find its way. Particularly if a death is sudden, unexpected, or violent. Then their funerals act like beacons to them, guiding them to their gates. Like what Retaka tried yesterday for that missing child. Or, some linger untimely in the world of matter due to some task left undone. I heard of one woman who haunted the staircase on which she'd died, resisting her funeral rites, because her murderer had escaped accusation. When the crime was brought home to him, she allowed herself to pass, fortunately before she became so eroded there was no longer enough of her left to assent."

"I remember you once told me about the fellow whose soul was imprisoned in the knife that had killed him, but I thought that was a piece of shamanic magic. You don't suspect that here, do you?"

"No. But there was another, who'd been buried suddenly under a landslide and lingered almost too long. In all but name he was a saint of the Son of Autumn, and I think his soul was being materially supported by his living loyal dogs who refused to abandon him. Even then, he wouldn't leave till he'd been assured his beloved beasts would be cared for. For that, the god waited on him."

"In Person?"

"Very. As unmistakable as our experiences with the saint of Pef."

Alixtra's mouth moved in an unvoiced, impressed *oh*.

"I've never heard of such a thing being connected to the Bastard's death magic, though. Have you, Des?"

"Not in my experience," she said aloud. Which was very much longer than Pen's.

"So," Pen continued, "what we have out there is a variation, or concatenation, so unlikely, or unlucky, it was never taught about in my seminary, but plainly not impossible. As we just saw."

Alixtra frowned, turned her head, cast her Sight through the wall that would be translucent to it at the two souls in the next room—young Arra's range of perception was much shorter than Des's, but enough for this. "The ghost is diffuse, unclear. I thought fresh unsundered souls kept more form?"

"Starting to fray, yes. But mostly, I think…confused. Frightened. Unable to assent because, maybe… too young to understand?"

She pursed her lips, blew out troubled breath. "Have we found Retaka's missing Agno?"

"Gods. I don't know whether to hope yes or hope no."

"If so, why didn't Learned Retaka's funeral rites yesterday draw him out?"

"I don't know." *Yet.*

The souls of children dying before the age of any speech or understanding, or ability to assent—stillbirths, newborns, infants, toddlers—were normally taken up by the Mother of Summer, possibly Her greatest mercy in the world, for all that people focused more upon Her gifts of healing. Older children were taken in by the god natural to their age and sex, the Daughter of Spring or the Son of Autumn, though sometimes the Bastard. In all cases funerals for the young were attended to with the greatest care by Temple servants, and not just for the solace of bereaved parents. It was somewhat the same anxious impulse, Penric supposed, by which whole villages turned out to help search for a lost child.

A soul caught by death upon that awkward border between mercy and understanding…blast it, no, the child might not understand, but the *gods* should. There was some other hitch, Pen began to suspect, connected with this peculiar occupation.

"We need to persuade that soul out of that body, I think."

Des snorted and put in aloud, "How? Not evicting it by cremation, I trust. 'Hello, Otzos Soudei, we're complete strangers from the Temple and we want to burn your bereaved mad sister and only surviving kin alive for reasons entirely invisible to you.' I can't think that would go well."

"Noooo," said Pen in heartfelt agreement. "Very much not. I suspect it would also cause great extra distress to the occupying soul, which is existing on a delicate boundary right now. ...I'm probably going to have to, hm, lie."

Alixtra raised bemused eyebrows at him. "Ours is the god of lies. Surely that's allowed to you, in a good cause."

"It may navigate us through the immediate shoals, but there'll be a price in due course—"

His dithering was cut short by Otzos opening the chamber door and peering at them in mistrust. "What are you two doing so long there?" He caught sight of the mouse dangling from Alixtra's fingers, and his mouth twisted in repulsed bewilderment.

"Wrap that up in something. We may need it later to show," Pen murmured aside to her. She nodded and began to look around for a scrap of spare cloth. Pen took a breath and stepped forward. "I need to speak more to your sister."

Frowning, Otzos gave way. "You can try, but I haven't been able to get sense out of her for two days."

"I don't doubt you."

Pen reentered the first chamber to discover that not-Vissa had abandoned her chair for a crouch under the table. Her eyes gleamed in the shadows from a feral fall of hair again escaping her cap, and she continued to rock and whimper.

"She keeps climbing into things," Otzos complained. "Whether she fits or not. Like a cat. I've had to pull her out of chests three times. Here, come out from under there!"

He made to bend and drag her, but Penric fended him off. "Wait a bit."

Pen settled himself cross-legged on the floor in front of...her, for the moment. "Hello," he tried. "I'm Penric, and this is my demon Desdemona." Because the naked soul could perceive them both, in this state. "She's very tame. We're not going to hurt you." This won only a wary stare.

Des, are you getting any more detail? Age, sex, cause of death?

You can See everything I can. …Try the name.

Sundered or astray souls could not make sounds, that being a property of the world of matter, though their fading mouths could move if they still retained any capacity of language, and they sometimes made signs. The hospice ghost that had barged into Therneas and whatever was occupying not-Vissa could both of them make their filched bodies move and emit noises, though not-Vissa was better at it, actually producing words not just groans. Making *sense* was another issue. But hearing should still function…if not exactly through the ears.

"Agno?" Pen tried, his heart clenching. "Are you Agno?"

A jolt backward. Definitely a reaction. Not wanting it to be a *Yes* was pointless, because if it wasn't that lost child it was some other equal tragedy. This one, at least, they had a string upon, and Pen began to get a queasy feeling it wasn't by accident. His was the god of chance and mischance, after all. And the gods were parsimonious… *Am I conscripted as Your hands once more?*

"Agno, we want to help you get home. But you'll have to help us, too."

Whimpers.

"What are you *doing* down there?" demanded Otzos of Pen.

Penric sighed and swung around, mentally editing his response. "Your sister is possessed, I'm afraid."

"By a demon?" Otzos stepped back, face working in horror.

"You needn't sound so appalled," said Des a bit tartly. "It can be quite a nice thing to have happen, with the right person and the right demon."

"Hush, Des," said Pen taking back control of his tongue. "Though if it had been, there is a saint of my Order who could remove it."

Can *demons ever possess corpses?* he thought to ask her.

No, she said shortly. *There is no nourishment to be had from them.*

So what is upholding this stray soul?

Nothing. It's upholding the corpse, and being drained thereby.

That's not good news.

No.

"She has become possessed by a ghost," said Pen, leaving out the *she died first in a sacrificial rite* part for now. "Quite a new one, not yet sundered, but badly astray. In order to bring it to its god I think what we need to do first is find the body." Had this child-ghost found Vissa a particularly congenial refuge because of the boy-shaped hole left in her heart? Pen would hesitate to advance the notion.

Otzos stared at Pen as if he'd gone mad alongside his sister.

Alixtra meanwhile also hunkered down next to Pen. Not-Vissa abruptly turned her attention to this new feature, reaching out a hand in wonder. "Wha's *that*? Wan' pet…"

Which finished any doubt as to whether this was a child-ghost. Whether the slurred and fractured speech was an effect of trying to animate the corpse, or innate to a young child, or both, was anyone's guess. But this artless attraction to a novel animal reminded Pen all too piercingly of his daughter Rina. *Safe at home, safe at home,* he told himself sternly, quashing the urge to run there and check. *Attend now to the child right here.*

"This is Arra," said Alixtra, putting a tone of practiced maternal kindness into her softened voice. "She used to be a weasel. I don't think you can touch her, though."

The hand wavered. "Does bites?"

"No."

Not-Vissa settled for staring. Making no effort to leave the shelter of the table-cave.

Pen sat back and thought.

"Right," he said at last. "So we know a few things to go on with, and have some good guesses. Four-year-old boy, resident in this neighborhood, last seen alive about two weeks ago, though that may not be exactly when he died. The body will be nearby, but hidden from view in some unlikely place, because all the obvious and easy ones will already have been searched. Trapped, jammed, stuck in some way, or he could have wriggled himself out." *Dark*, he thought unbidden. Logical, but that felt like more than a guess.

Alixtra frowned. "Second sight may find a living person even behind a barrier. A corpse is no more distinctive than any other inert matter. It will blend with its background until we're right up on it."

Pen nodded. "So we need to get closer." His eye fell on not-Vissa. "Ghosts have led searchers to their bodies before. As we've witnessed."

"You witnessed," Alixtra corrected mildly. "I was just told about it."

"Yes, whatever. That ghost was very fresh, very angry, very determined. This one... I'm not so sure." He peered doubly at not-Vissa, who peered back—singly—in vague disinterest, but in curiosity at Alixtra. The ghost seemed far more interested in the weasel-demon than in its human interrogators.

"Agno, could you come out and help us?" Pen tried. "Please?" Not-Vissa shook her head and edged back further into her makeshift cave, mouth going stubborn. Impasse.

Alixtra pursed her lips and leaned forward, saying in that same soft tone, "Agno, would you like to take my weasel-demon out for a walk?"

A blink of interest. The shuffle reversed. "Can I...?"

"Yes, but you have to get dressed first." Not-Vissa cast her a doubtful look; so did Otzos. "I'll—Arra and I will help you."

After a long moment of consideration, not-Vissa nodded and crawled out. She rose clumsily, and Alixtra caught her elbow before she could fall. "Let's go into your room and find your outdoor clothes and shoes," Alixtra went on, guiding her into the next chamber. Pen tapped his student gently atop the head in passing in silent approval, which made her lips quirk. Otzos twitched, torn between wanting to supervise and leaving the woman to the woman.

"I'll go out with you," he said, his tone truculent as if expecting an argument. Pen could picture the exasperating wrangles he'd been having for the past two days with the person he'd thought was his elder sister. "I'm not leaving her alone like this with strangers."

"Of course," said Pen. Full, wet dark had fallen outside. "You can carry the lantern."

Otzos swallowed unneeded protest, and gave a sharp nod.

Pen continued, "Two days ago, when your sister…took her turn for the worse, was it any special anniversary? I know it's not the date your poor nephew died, nor the date of his funeral."

Otzos shook his head. "No. It was Kyem's birthday."

"Ah."

"It stirred her all up again. She used to ask, 'Why did the gods give him to me if they were only going to take him away?' Learned Retaka never had an answer."

"No…" said Pen slowly, "that's backward. The gods do not give us our children. We give our children to the gods."

Otzos frowned, thrown.

Pen considered all the questions he'd been planning to ask this family, most of them now answered by implication at least. "The, ah, other reason I came was to find out if there's anything you remember Kyem saying about his Customs house colleague, Master Therneas."

"Therneas?" Otzos squinted. "Name rings a bell. They didn't any of them come to Kyem's funeral, though, which made Vissa so angry."

"Kyem had no special complaints of him?"

"Not as I recall. If he's the one I'm thinking of, Kyem thought he was a bit of a shuffler. They weren't friends."

"So you and your sister never had any clues at all about who might have laid those anonymous charges against your nephew?"

Otzos's lips thinned. "No. Or I would have strangled the rotten fishbreath toad myself." He looked up suddenly. "*Has* anything more been found out?"

"A large hoard of coin stolen from the Customs house was discovered this afternoon under the floorboards of Therneas's chambers. You may be sure some keen-eyed people from the duke's treasury will be going over records of every transaction he had a hand in for the past nine years. I suspect they're going to find out a great deal."

Otzos gasped. "I know Therneas was promoted to Master in Kyem's place. Was it him? Was it *him*? Has he been arrested?" He lurched as though planning to run out to the duke's prison and commit mayhem right now.

"He's dead. Which is how I...how his chambers came to be searched."

Otzos subsided in frustration. "If it was him, *him*, I swear I'll go to his funeral just to piss on his corpse. Oh, I have to tell Vissa—" He stopped.

"Not yet," said Pen. "Please wait till she is in a less disturbed state of mind." Which was going to be never. ...Or maybe now, in their god's hands. In light of all He had given her in answer to her prayer so far, adding *profound solace* to the list seemed a short stretch.

Pen wondered if that anonymous note was still in the Customs house archives, or if Therneas had abused his powers as Master to abstract and burn it, the secret slander made yet more impossible to track back to its source. Nothing left for even the most diligent servants of Winter's justice to lay hands upon. *No recourse* indeed. Save for One. Pen's teeth set.

Alixtra and not-Vissa reemerged from the other chamber, not-Vissa now dressed in street wear, with a cloak pinned around her. She was earnestly leading Alixtra by a cord tied around the latter's wrist, like children playing puppy. Not-Vissa had cheered considerably, seeming eager to go out.

"Alixtra, you're brilliant," Pen murmured to her as she was tugged toward the door.

A brief strained grin. "No, just experienced with four-year-old boys. Which turns out to be how to treat her. ...Him." She added under her breath, "Her body's quite cool, and she can hardly work her hands. Stiffening. I don't think we have much time left."

Pen nodded grimly, catching up his own cloak to follow them onto the gallery. Otzos trailed, confused and disbelieving, holding their lit lantern that only he would need. But giving him a task seemed more likely to assure his cooperation than yet more bewildering explanations.

THEIR BIZARRE procession then began what seemed to Pen an utterly random jaunt around the maze-like neighborhood. They passed a few folks carrying out errands or hurrying home by lantern light through the narrow, wet streets and alleys, but everyone who could be inside, was.

Getting probably-Agno to *want* to find his body was the catch. Leading questions elicited nothing but vague distress. Pen and Alixtra both walked by Sight, faintly dizzied and finding plenty of live people behind the walls that lined the passages, but that wasn't what they sought.

By the second or third round through what proved a relatively limited area, the ghost was starting to grow bored with its game, and less responsive to Alixtra's coaxing. Pen made to go down a slightly wider street they hadn't yet traversed, its central gutter running a small stream that glimmered in the lantern glow.

Not-Vissa stopped short.

"No. Doan wanna."

Alixtra, leashed, obediently wheeled, but Pen said, "Wait."

He turned to their erratic guide. "Agno, why don't you want to go down that way?"

Pouting lip-jut. "Doan wanna."

Pen held up a hand to stay their progress, and explored it himself. High, plain walls lined this section, broken only by a few entryways closed for the night. No odd recesses or damaged spots where a small boy might delight to hide himself. No places to climb.

What he found instead was a loose grating over a hole down into the old Cedonian sewer system.

He extended Des's Sight. The drain here dropped about six feet to reach the brick-lined channel that descended to the river. It wasn't one of the accesses made for workmen to get in to clean or effect repairs, being barely large enough to admit a skinny person and without handholds; it was only intended to accept the water and waste from the gutter. Fairly unappetizing waste, most of the time. Pen eyed the opening without favor, then walked back up the block.

"Otzos. Do you have some rope at home? And a sheet, I think. One from Vissa's bed would do."

"What for?"

"There's a drop into the drains along that way. I'm going down to look. I'd like to be able to get back out, eh?"

"Rope I have. But why a sheet?"

"If I find what I think is there, it's not going to be in good condition, and I'd rather not sacrifice my cloak."

"Well, you can borrow it for this"—a pained look as he perhaps visualized what Pen did—"though I'm not sure we'll want it back. You'll still have your cloak, but what's Vissa supposed to sleep on?"

Pen grimaced. "Can we deal with that later, please?"

Otzos made a frustrated noise, but, after assurances that they wouldn't let his distraught sister wander off, he did start back toward his home. Alixtra meanwhile finally persuaded the hesitant not-Vissa to follow her and Pen down the length of the cobbled street. There was definitely something Agno didn't like around here...

They fetched up back at the drain. Pen pulled out the grating.

"Are you going to fit in there?" Alixtra asked in concern.

"Yes, just. Des checked."

"I'm smaller—should I go down?"

"No. I'm used to cadavers. I once taught anatomy to the medical apprentices back in Martensbridge, did I ever say? In winter, by preference, but we were occasionally brought unclaimed corpses at other times of the year." And they didn't both need the lingering picture in their heads of what Pen was increasingly sure he was going to find.

Pen took off and folded his good cloak, laying it aside, and, after an instant's reflection, also the white tunic of his vestments, leaving him in his shirt. He considered whether he wanted to spare his shoes as well.

No, said Des firmly, sounding quite maternal. *You're not taking us down into that muck barefoot, to step on not-even-the-gods-know-what and get filth in the cuts. Make the Order buy you new shoes if you have to. You're doing this for them.*

Not really for them, Pen thought, and received back a sense of reluctant concession.

Pen tied the sash from his tunic back around his waist, sat by the opening, promptly soaking the back of his trousers, and stuck his feet down. A shift, a push, and a wriggle had him hanging by his hands. He'd climbed through tighter spaces before, but he'd been escaping a Cedonian dungeon at the time. He let go, and after a shoulder-scraping drop to slow himself, landed in cold water up to his calves.

He had to allow, this time of year the city drains were as rinsed-out as they ever became. At the end of the hot summer, he'd have been landing knee-high in a substance with the consistency of potter's clay and the stench of a privy. And lumps. There were still lumps, but not as many.

The brick-lined part of the drain was the height of an average Orban workman, which made it a head too short for Penric. He stooped uncomfortably and followed the water in its sluggish downstream course for perhaps two blocks. Another channel joined it from the side, smaller, opening at a higher level, creating a splashing fall. Some rats lurked up it, but Pen didn't need a chaos dump for Des's magics yet, and he let them live. They were almost out from under the Olive Street neighborhood, he thought, so he turned around and tried the other direction, passing again under the opening by which he'd entered.

A smell of decay permeated the dank air, but it was from a dead cat, rat-gnawed. Turnabout, Pen supposed. He pushed the bloating thing into the current with his foot to float slowly away. The roof grew lower as he went upstream, and his stoop became a crouch. His nose found his quarry before Des did.

Yes, she agreed bleakly, as they came up on another raised side-channel, waist-high, blocked by trash. And by one other thing.

Oh, little mouse, thought Pen. *However did you get yourself stuck in there.* He tied his sash around his lower face and bent closer.

The small body had climbed, or possibly floated, into the opening, but in any case was wedged there now. He reached out his hand, not yet touching, and let his physician's Sight descend into the remains as he'd done for some hundreds of bodies, living or dead, before. No broken bones. Pre-death lacerations few, but now he wished he'd killed those rats. Liquid in the disintegrating lungs disclosed the tale— trapped and drowned when the waters rose following some downpour. Pen remembered the flash floods in the spring mountains of the Cantons; the end would have been sudden. Early. A mercy. *But not bloody much of one.* Pen wanted to weep. If the cloth that guarded his mouth and nose absorbed more than his breath, who was to know?

You're done here, Pen, Des told him gently. *Go get the sheet and the rope.*

ANOTHER SPLASHING, sucking trudge back to his entry point, negotiations called up it, and Pen's supplies were lowered on the promised rope. Pen dug with his hands into the mucky detritus jamming the blocked passage and gently loosened the small abandoned husk, which came out still all of a piece thank the gods, and wrapped the sheet around it, folding in the ends, and around again before securing it firmly with his sash. It made a sturdy shroud and a tidy package to carry upon his shoulder, all too much like he'd carry a live child. More called directions, and his package went up by rope, pulled by Otzos and Alixtra, slipping easily through the vertical conduit. Pen's own exit took more effort, but he was soon splayed on the wet cobbles, catching his breath. He rolled over and reseated the grating, rinsed his hands as best he could in the gutter water, shook them, and climbed to his feet.

"You were right," said Otzos, staring down at the shrouded shape in the glow of his lantern and clearly reviewing everything else he'd doubted about Penric. He wasn't regretting the use of his sheet anymore, either, Pen noted.

"Yes. Unfortunately." Pen would have been a lot happier to be like Retaka, imagining the lost child taken in like a stray cat by some kindly old woman.

There is Another Who waits to take him in, Des reminded him.

Yes. Why isn't it happening yet?

Proximity alone, it seemed, wasn't going to supply the key. Not-Vissa hung back, eyes twitching, looking vaguely around anywhere but down. Pen tried to lead her nearer by taking her hand, which was colder and stiffer than his own, but she jerked it back and whimpered.

"To the Temple," Pen decided. "If only because Learned Retaka needs to know all this as soon as may be, and it will be her task to tell Agno's family." Not his part, please his god and all others. He'd done enough of that back during his physician's service in Martensbridge. The memories threatened to crowd up like mephitic smoke from a mine fire.

Steady on, soothed Des.

Right.

He bent and hoisted his package once more, leading off. Otzos, and Alixtra carrying Pen's folded cloak and tunic, followed with not-Vissa reluctantly stumbling between them. They were close, he thought, to the confused ghost having spent so much of its substance on this occupation that there would not be enough left to assent, will or nil. Like a hermit crab trying to carry a shell too heavy for it, and dying of exhaustion on an unfriendly beach.

Thankfully Olive Street was only a few turns away, and they were soon at the temple doors once more, locked for the night. Pen popped the lock without hesitation. Inside, a dog began to bark frantically, the sharp echoes drawing nearer. Not-Vissa squeaked and hung back, but her guardians pulled her into the sanctuary, and Pen prudently swung the door shut again. A gesture, and Des's magic ignited every altar candle and wall sconce in the place, and the plinth fire for good measure, rolling back the cold night shadows and replacing them with the warmth of a welcoming hearth.

From the back entry, the dog bolted toward them, its claws scrabbling across the floor mosaics. It was a big, healthy beast, chestnut coat brushed to gleaming, the barks issuing from between bright white teeth deep and resonant, echoing through the arching chamber. Only its wildly wagging tail belied the general impression of ferocity. It was chased by the temple's groom, still dressed for the day in tunic, trousers, and brown tabard, bellowing at it to

Sit!, a command it ignored as it bounced up to greet the visitors. Not-Vissa screamed and tried to climb Alixtra. They both stumbled to the floor.

The dog would have fallen upon them, trying to savage them with…big wet licks, apparently, but its groom caught its collar and dragged it back, swearing at it in a way unbecoming to a holy animal. Thwarted, it whined and nosed Penric's bundle which he'd laid down upon the tiles, licking at it instead. Not-Vissa-Agno started crying hysterically, and the dog flattened its belly to the pavement, ears drooping.

"He's afraid of dogs," Alixtra shot over her shoulder at Pen, and at Otzos kneeling down to try to help soothe…whoever he thought he was soothing. "I think he must have been bitten once."

"But Vissa likes dogs," Otzos said, bewildered. "So do I." Taking his tone as invitation, the dog belly-scooted over to him, and he automatically lifted a hand to pet it.

Hurrying into this standoff scuffed Learned Retaka, hair swinging in a braid down her back, slippers on her bare feet, her nightdress covered with her hastily-donned five-colored robe around which she was tying a sash. "*What* is happening out here?" Her gaze skipped past the Soudei siblings, Alixtra, and

Penric, to catch on the pale bundle on the floor before Autumn's altar, so obviously a shrouded small body.

The breath she'd drawn in went out of her in a pained, apprehensive *Oh.* "Five gods spare us, Learned Penric, what have you found?" She made the tally sign; he returned her a wave of his thumb past his mouth, not touching his lips, because his hands still stank of sewer muck and worse. Along with the rest of him.

"Your missing Agno, I fear. Could you identify his face?"

"I think so…"

Penric knelt and carefully spread back just enough of the cloth to reveal stiff, still features and a wisp of dark hair, leaving the rest of the horror to its privacy. Retaka bent and peered, her mouth tight. "I think so. His family would be certain. I'll send for them at once."

"Hold up just a bit on that."

"But—"

"I understand, but something else must be accomplished first."

Retaka's brow wrinkled. "But why didn't his rites draw him to his god yesterday? Oh no, the poor lad isn't sundered, is he? A child like that? Can you tell?" Her shocked earnest gaze lifted to Penric.

"Not quite, but we're much too close. I brought his soul along with us. He's right over there." Pen pointed to the still-weeping not-Vissa, clutching Alixtra and Otzos and casting fearful glances at the contrite hound. "Unfortunately, it seems the child was terrified of dogs."

And possibly of what was backing the holy creature up from behind, a vast hovering Presence that even Penric would be unable to look directly in the Face. And they'd met before. Des was rigid within him, unable to flee but scorning to cower, a sure sign of imminent immanence.

Pen spread his hand over his heart. *I've brought You another of Your straying boys, Lord of Autumn. What do You want to do?*

Whoever might hear the answer, it was not Pen. *No hands but ours.* No wits, either? He sat back on the cold pavement, haunches still damp. "Do you have any other holy animal that might serve? Something small and gentle. I don't think the god will be fussy at this late hour, so we should not be, either."

The overwhelmed Retaka motioned to her groom. "Find another animal in the shed. Take this one out with you."

"But he's a good dog," the groom protested. "One of the best!"

"I'm sure he is," said Pen, trying not to be half-maddened at yet another delaying argument *now*. "Yet he will not do. Fetch another. Wait. I'll go with you." He clambered up.

He followed the groom out under the colonnade of the rear courtyard, tapping a tense foot as the fellow stopped to light a lantern, and went through with him when he unlocked the side gate to the shed. The space seemed divided equally between the sacred and the practical. Pen cast a vague salute in passing at the wire-netted stall that held the Bastard's gull and a large green bird, probably for the Mother, though one of that trio of nanny goats might serve either for Her or for milk and cheese. Or both. The gold-coin eyes of a big black cat, perching freely on a railing, gleamed at him. The groom stopped before an array of rabbit hutches.

"These are the littlest animals we have," he told Pen, "but we raise them mainly for eating, and the pelts." He held up his lantern to shine light upon the twitching, furry inhabitants.

Pen let his hand trail down the row, trying to keep himself open to suggestion, not easy with his teeming mind. This day had been a waking nightmare, and doubtless the fount of many sleeping nightmares to come. Maybe…just…there.

"Yes," he told the rust-brown rabbit as he extracted it from its batch of young siblings. "You'll do. And if you don't, I swear I'll eat you myself."

This threat seemed to pass over the flattening tender ears as he settled it in the crook of his arm and petted it. Maybe just as well. The tomcat jumped down and trotted at his heels as they trooped back into the temple, whether in hopes of entertaining prey or for some greater purpose Pen declined to guess.

Pen found himself marching back into the sanctuary unable to decide if he should address the rabbit, Autumn's altar, or the air. The room felt tilted, or maybe it was just him. He wheeled to face the altar. The rabbit began to tremble.

"*This* time, don't come bounding up to him as a great drooling dog bigger than he is." *As big as the world, no wonder.* "He never wanted to deny You; he was just frightened. Come *smaller*. Gentler. Or else yield him back to Your Mother."

Pen, are you snapping at a god…?

I've had a long day.

The black cat, Pen noted from the corner of his eye, jumped up on Winter's altar and sat with its sleek tail wrapping its forepaws, regarding the whole affair with shrewd interest. The golden eyes slowly blinked. Bearing witness for what must come next, Pen thought distractedly. As well He should, in this His season.

He walked back over to not-Vissa, still seated on the floor quietly crying between Alixtra and Otzos, who was clumsily attempting to comfort her. He plunked down cross-legged and took a deep breath, struggling for a self-control that had never been more important. It would be entirely hypocritical to demand of a god something he was unwilling to deliver himself, after all. Lowering his voice to tenderness, he said, "Agno? How would you like to hold this rabbit, instead? Be very careful with it, now. It's afraid. You know how that feels. But it's quite soft. You can pet it."

The child looked out through Vissa's eyes for the last time, drawn, raising up her stiff hands. They were too clumsy now to hold the animal, so Pen guided it and them down to a safe platform on not-Vissa's lap. A tremulous, wondering smile turned the leaden lips as he felt through the thick red fur. "Oh," he said.

Just that. It took so little, in the end, this assent. Pen had the sense of a warm copper light enveloping rabbit, boy, world. And then gone.

That at least. That at least. Pen thought he was crying. He seemed to be shuddering. He wasn't sure.

There is no least *about it*, said Des, sounding as shattered as he felt.

Vissa Soudei's emptied corpse slumped over into her startled brother's arms.

OTZOS SHOOK her. "Vissa." Shook her again. "Vissa!" His third call of her name turned into a scream partway through, echoing around the sanctuary like bone scraping on stone. Because he was old and experienced enough to know death when he saw it, his fourth hoarse cry held no form at all, there being no words to contain such comprehension. Incomprehension, as he turned his stunned face to Penric, sitting nearby on the mosaics.

And now the payment comes due, Pen thought dizzily.

"You said getting rid of the ghost possessing her would fix her! You *said*."

"No. I said that had to be done first, before anything else. Which was true. The child's soul was close to inadvertent sundering, the most urgent part of the puzzle to solve."

"She's dead!"

"She died two nights ago, in a rite and prayer and payment to the white god for justice beyond all other recourse, offering up her own soul as surety. Death magic. She worked death magic. Which was what that dead white mouse in her room was all about, and the remains of the candle you probably found on her floor. And was what killed Therneas, if it's any consolation to you." Not much, Pen suspected.

Otzos's mouth remained agape, less in shock and disbelief than a temporary inability to muster an army of words strong enough to attack. "You knew? You knew *all this time?*"

"I knew immediately, before we even found the mouse and the candle wax. Death magic is not a rite we of my Order talk about, for a lot of practical reasons. How your sister found out about it, I don't know."

Spinners' gossip, marketplace storytellers, dim memories of spooky nursery tales? Certainly not from the sort of restricted scholarly writings Pen was familiar with. Recently learned, or lately remembered? Maybe this hadn't been her first attempt, either. It would be the height of folly to imagine all cases of death magic must be the same.

"People who study accounts before trying it tend to bring in more elaborations, all of them pointless, it turns out," Pen went on. "Vissa must have recreated it on her own, from a whisper of rumor and her own tormented soul. The death of the mouse opened a thread of a channel, enough for the god to grasp and spin up her desire. The candle…was for light, I suppose. And for honor."

Otzos's breath came in gasps. "I would have killed him for her myself! Curse it, Vissa!" He shook the body in his arms as if he could still force it to understand.

"Killed who?" Pen said wearily. "Neither you nor she nor anyone else knew who'd laid that anonymous lie. So she turned to the One Who must."

"Why didn't you tell me at once?"

"With what seemed your sister still talking and moving around? Not eating though, I expect."

"I couldn't make her eat. Or drink. I tried. I was so *worried*…"

"Would you have believed me? Earlier?"

Otzos glared as though he wanted to stand up, march over, and clout Penric in the face. Pen declined to stand up to invite him.

"It's the sort of choice physicians must sometimes make, when too many patients arrive at once for their hands to hold, by chance or from some disaster." One of so many reasons why he no longer practiced the trade. "Army physicians on the battlefield, certainly. Who can be treated, who can be held aside, who...must be let go. Your sister's soul had already departed, by her own volition and her god's favor. Hers wasn't a decision that any argument or explanation could change, but delay could have been fatal to Agno's spirit. So. I'm telling you now instead."

Otzos's fists did not unclench, but neither did his jaw. Warrior words briefly suspended, good. Pen wasn't sure how many more thrusts he could bear. ...Well. All of them, at need.

"Why...what...how..." Retaka began, hovering appalled. "So is Vissa Soudei *sundered*? Taken by the death demon to oblivion, the way they say?"

"No. Her formal funeral rites will soon tell you of her godly destination, I'm sure." *If you won't take my word for it, and why should you?* "She'd have wanted to follow her son into the white god's arms. And the god, it seems, does look out for all His children. At the end." Pen considered. "Therneas must have been obliterated at once, though. No god is going to sign for him."

Otzos shook his head, not in protest but more like a bear assaulted by bees, staggered by too many stings from too many directions.

"Little Agno went with his big Brother, as we all just saw." Such an active willful child, no wonder he'd appealed to Autumn. In both senses. "Though you'll want to repeat the rites to reassure his family, in due course. I don't imagine the god will object. You can likely use the dog then. Oh…" Pen crawled over, prudently staying out of the orbit of a swing from Otzos, and reached for the rabbit, which had tumbled out of Vissa's skirts and lay still and limp on the tiles.

He picked it up and stroked the soft fur. Rabbits were frail creatures. "Poor sainted thing. Was bearing a god too much for you? Don't blame you. It would be too much for me." He lifted it toward the nonplussed Retaka. "Here. This should probably be buried with Agno. Not skinned and eaten, please. For all that Autumn is also the god of the hunt."

Being handed a dead rabbit, it seemed, was the least of her night's confusions, for she accepted it half-unseeing. "Why..." she began, stopped. Tried again. "We're taught in seminary that rites of death magic almost never work. Why this one?"

Alixtra, who had stepped back with her arms folded when Vissa had sagged over, tilted her face toward Pen in equal interest.

"Truly? I don't know. I'd like to know, both in this case and in general. Outwardly, the crimes answered for and those not can look similar, so the reasons must be sought inwardly, in the hearts that only the gods can know in full. It seems to me the target must be a soul who was headed for sundering already, rank and spoiled enough to be denied by every god. Which happens, if not as often as people's enemies might wish, so no great mystery. But there's another half to it, the soul of the supplicant. That... I need to think more about."

But not tonight, suggested Des. *You're spent.*

And cold and wet and stinking of sewage and death, yes. Never had he wanted a hot bath and Nikys more, in that order. "I'm afraid I'm too tired to debate fine points of theology just now," he said apologetically to Retaka. "We can talk another time. And you have two funerals to plan. I'll get out of your way, eh?"

"I must send a temple servant to tell Agno's family what you found. Or, no, I'd better get dressed and go myself. Or best to wait till morning?" She looked to Pen as if to a senior advisor, fair enough.

If it were my child… Pen's mind shied from the vision. But, "Tonight. I think. They won't be sleeping anyway."

Retaka nodded. "Shall you wait for them? I'm sure they'll want to say thank you."

"Ah, no. I can tell you with great certainty what they will say"—*because it's nothing I'm not saying to myself*—"and I don't really want to linger to hear it."

Retaka blinked. "What?"

Pen's lips curled in something remote from a smile. "*Where were you two weeks ago?* In fact, you don't need to mention me at all. The body was found by a worker inspecting the drains, and he left without giving his name. That would do."

Retaka opened her mouth to protest, given pause by Alixtra's raised hand and headshake.

"Where were you two *nights* ago?" said Otzos through set teeth. "Where were the gods? *Again?*"

"One, at least, came to your sister, at her invitation. Invocation. Command, call, I profoundly don't know what passed between them. And neither do you."

"Learned," said Alixtra quietly. "I think we'd better go. These people have things to do."

"Yes." *Please.*

She rummaged in her surplice. "Then this should probably be buried with Vissa Soudei," she said, withdrawing a kerchief wrapping the dead mouse. She laid it gingerly at the corpse's feet, like an offering. Yes, Pen imagined she'd want that out of her clothing at the first opportunity. Couldn't blame her. She frowned. "Or should she be burned? Could her body be occupied again? By some other sundered ghost?"

"Oh," said Pen. *I have no idea.*

Des took over for him, saying firmly, "Burn her remains tonight, if possible. Just in case. You don't want to go through all this again."

"I am sorry," Pen continued to Otzos. "You can have a proper ceremony in the temple later, with her urn, and all the funeral animals, and it will work just as well. You can take as much time as you need to arrange things."

"What things? What things? There's only her and me left." He rocked, rocking her, and whispered, "Only me."

Learned Retaka knelt beside him and cautiously touched his shoulder. "And me. Us. All this temple's servants will help you. It's our task."

He made to violently shrug her off. Her mouth set in distress for his distress, her hand falling away.

Pen climbed to his feet and jerked his head; he, Retaka, and Alixtra moved away to speak in lowered voices by the Bastard's niche. The black cat from his perch on the Father of Winter's altar, Pen noted, was still watching it all through grave gold eyes.

"Let him be for a little," he advised Retaka, with a glance over at Otzos and the stiff burden he had still not let down. "While you go make the other provisions. By the time you get back, he'll have had time to settle."

"He shouldn't be left alone like this."

On a cold stone floor surrounded by corpses. "Oh, agreed."

"Will you stay with him?"

Pen shook his head. "Anyone but me would be a better comfort right now. He's right that this wasn't the ending that I"—*led him*—"allowed him to expect, and that fault is entirely mine. Fetch a dedicat or an acolyte. They won't need to do much but just…be there."

After a moment, she nodded grimly, and went to the rear premises to start alerting or waking her people. Like the Mother's Order, a local temple had to be ready for supplicants at all times, day or night. Death did not keep a merchant's hours, after all, nor did other emergencies.

As soon as he was assured of the arrival of the other temple servants, Pen withdrew with Alixtra to the street. The wind had died. A cold fog was rising from the pavement, snaking through the alleys.

"I'll walk you back to the chapterhouse," he told his student. Any thief or drunkard trying to accost her would be in for a deeply unpleasant surprise from Arra, but it was better not to be accosted at all. At least the hypothetical threats might think again before trying two people in company.

"I'm not sure but what I should be walking you back to your wife," she said. "Are you going to be all right?"

"Mm," he said vaguely. Then, "Hm? I took no injuries. Apart from a few scrapes. But can you carry my cloak and tunic? I don't want to put them back on over my grime."

She accepted the bundle without argument beyond a disapproving eyebrow-flick for his exposure to the night air. They turned along the street. The trip back across town, Sight drawn in and quiescent now, was otherwise blessedly quiet. Meditative or exhausted, take a pick.

"Will you want me tomorrow?" she asked when they arrived back at the chapterhouse gate.

"Not sure. There are still some trailing ends to tuck in. I'll send for you if I need you."

"Mind you do. I want to know about those ends."

Pen's voice lightened. "There will certainly be a report to write. That's something I could usefully show you how to do."

Heartened by her dry laugh, he went his way. The walk from the chapterhouse to his own street was short.

He went around back in the dark to the kitchen door, rapping on it till he roused a sleepy Lin.

"Can you hand me out soap and a towel? I'm going to strip and wash up out here at the well first, before I come in." And leave his clothing and shoes out here for later, too. "And put water on to boil for tea. And anything else hot you can think of."

By the time he returned from the well, shivering and dripping, his warm wife was greeting him at the door, with warm garments, slippers, and worried kisses. "God's teeth, you're chilled right through. Des, how did you allow that?"

"Long story," said Des. "Make him tell it."

Nikys drew him into the light, searching his face, her eyes narrowing at whatever she found there. "May you tell it?"

"I can tell you. Everything."

"Anything," she assured him, and his heart did not doubt it.

By the time he was full of hot tea and the reheated supper set aside for him earlier, he was empty of words, and she pulled him upstairs by candlelight.

"I want to look in on Rina first," he murmured.

She nodded understanding. "Just don't wake Mother."

Idrene dozed far more lightly than her grand-daughter, so Pen only stood in silence at the half-opened door to their shared room. Rina slept sweetly in the faint glimmer from the candle, and the keener view by Sight. Breathing. Whole. Pen tried not to remember the boy in the sewer, barely older than her, and failed. He closed the door quietly.

In their own room, he stared down at infant Wyn in his cradle with like contemplation. Only temporarily asleep, no doubt, before he woke and demanded his mother's attention and breast once more in the fruitful round of his day, urgently growing. He, too, would soon be walking, running. Getting into things. Pen watched him for a long time.

Des. How are we all going to survive this? Half a dozen of you were mothers. Do you know, can you even say?

Her reply was slow, sighed. *One hour at a time. And that's all the truth I know to tell you.*

"I'd sent Lin up with the warming pan to heat the sheets," Nikys murmured to Pen at last. "Come to bed before they get cold again."

"Bless Lin," Pen agreed, and followed.

PEN WOKE slow and late the next morning, rolling over to find Nikys had thoughtfully slipped out earlier with Wyn before his morning baby-demands could wake his papa. He heaved himself up with a groan, mentally reorganizing his day. It would probably be well to pay a visit to Master Tolga first, to report yesterday's findings and check on his uncanny non-patient. He dressed to go out, descending to the kitchen to seek blessed tea and something to eat.

There he found Idrene placating a fussy grandson on her shoulder, and Rina playing on the floor by the warmth of the ceramic stove, a new addition imported from the Weald that had gratified Lin and Nikys enormously. Pen just thought it was safer than the open fireplace. He had to forage his own breakfast, though, as Idrene informed him that those principal cooks had gone out together on an errand.

"I hope Nikys gets back soon," said Idrene. "I think Wyn is getting hungry again, and is about to share his displeasure." For all that she seemed an older, taller, thinner version of her daughter, this was one task for which she could not substitute.

Fortunately, before Wyn could begin exercising his gratifyingly healthy lungs, Nikys and Lin breezed into the kitchen, pink-cheeked and bright-eyed from the morning chill, setting down market baskets and putting aside their cloaks. Wyn, spotting his own second breakfast impending, raised and turned his head, a new skill, and emitted some easy-to-interpret yammers.

"Yes, yes," said his fond mama. "I hear you. But I have something for your papa first."

"A kiss, I trust," murmured Pen, rising to greet her.

"That as well." She escaped his embrace to dig in her basket and withdraw something wrapped in a familiar scrap of paper, spreading it out on the table. "Is this what you were looking for?"

Pen bent to see. Upon the sketch of the cloak pin now sat its bronze original—the taverner had remembered it clearly, apparently. "My word! Wherever did you find that?"

Nikys grinned, dimples flashing, pleased with her successful surprise. "Thinking about where your Master Therneas's clothing might have gone, I remembered a used-clothing merchant down by the harbor. Ox Street. Lin goes there sometimes."

Pen's brows drew in. "Does our household need to buy used clothing?"

"Mostly, I take old things there the mistresses give me to sell," said Lin, "though sometimes there are"—a slight smile, shared by all three women present and possibly Des—"*bargains.*"

Nikys continued, "The proprietress didn't re-member any good green cloak coming in like the one you described to me last night, but she did have this cloak pin that she'd bought day before yesterday."

Pen picked it up to stare. "Who *from?*"

"Happily, someone she knew. A couple of old wharf rats who live together down by the merchant docks, retired sailors she thinks. Their names were Symo and Laxo. She didn't know precisely where, but that should be enough for you two to find them, don't you think?"

"Certainly!"

So glad we married a clever woman, murmured Des, and *So am I*, agreed Pen.

"Yes, yes, Wyn," Nikys added, sitting down and accepting the increasingly peeved infant from Idrene. "You're next." He turned his face and rooted in her bodice.

Pen dropped kisses on both their heads, received with pleasure by one and suspicious irritation by the other—Wyn was not in a mood to share—and tossed the cloak pin in his hand. "Then I'll go down to the docks first. I meant to walk over and see Tolga, so I'll likely go to the Mother's Order next, depending. Not sure when I'll be back."

Nikys waved a yes-dear-go-earn-our-keep hand at him, and turned her attention to the pressing job in her lap, undoing her tunic. Pen hurried to find his cloak and other shoes, as yesterday's were still sitting dankly outside the back door.

As he exited onto the street, he let this new task fill his thoughts, and did not not *not* let his imagination spiral back to what Agno's family must be going through this morning. And Otzos Soudei. And young Retaka. She'd had a perfectly good seminary education, or she'd not have been appointed to Olive Street. Temple duties were well within her capacity. That didn't take magic, just dedication.

There is no magic that can fix this.

No, Des agreed.

THE MORNING had cleared to a pale cool blue, with the promise of welcome warmth in the afternoon, as Pen strode down to the harbor. The merchant docks lay beyond the duke's naval shipyard, unsurprisingly not far from the Customs house. They were backed up by a mess of marine-meets-shore clutter:

warehouses, stables for carters, a smithy, carpenters, sailmakers, a ropewalk, shacks housing bachelor sailors temporarily and stevedores permanently. A few inquiries brought Pen to one of these, a small ramshackle place tucked in like an afterthought between a ship chandler's and a pottery shop, looking cobbled together mainly from discarded boat planking, worm-bored.

Des had advised him to consider his garb carefully before going out. He needed to display his calling, certainly, but perhaps not intimidate. He wanted these men to talk to him as freely as possible. The one thing he knew for certain about them was that they were not murderers, though *thieves* was a good guess. Seagulls, maybe, picking over trash.

So he'd changed to his oldest vestments, on the verge of that shabby just before Nikys would whisk them away to be converted to some lesser use. No uncomfortable silver torc, reserved for the duke's and the archdivine's courts, or high holy days. Sash and silvered braids the same, though. If he found he needed to intimidate after all, Des had other resources for the task.

He rapped on the plank door, secured only with a rope latch. "Hello? Anyone home?"

Some shuffling from within. An eye peered blearily between the cracks of the boards. "Huh?" The door was swung open by a tattooed arm.

The man leaning on the portal had been tall and muscular, once. That body had collapsed in upon itself to a stringy toughness, as if mummified in life. Cheap copper rings in his ears had stained the lobes green. Gray hair was held back in a short switch.

He was joined in a moment by his companion, a shorter, skinnier, balding man. Ex-sailors very likely; a couple of missing fingers and finger-ends between them told of old mishaps with straining ropes. Their Cedonian skin coloration had been turned to leather by years in the sun. The shorter one's hands shook with tremor. They both smelled strongly of old wine, old sweat, old man.

"Good morning," Pen began in a friendly tone. "My name is Learned Penric kin Jurald, and I'm looking into something for the white god's Order." Not the magistrate, not the duke, for all that both impinged on this—those did not seem names to conjure with here. "I was hoping you might help me."

"And aren't you a sight," skinny and balding said, looking up at Pen with a sort of vague aesthetic appreciation.

"Wealdman," advised his big companion. "They get those bleached-out looks. Seen it on sailors from the far southern islands, too, all frozen up like their snow. Sky-colored eyes just like that."

"From the Cantons, actually," said Pen, hoping to move past this familiar fascination with his foreign looks. "But I've lived the past seven years in Vilnoc."

"Oh," said the big fellow, wisely. "'S why he can talk, Laxo, you bet?"

"Mm."

Making Symo the name of the big one. Progress?

Both of them seemed to be in that border state between drunk and hungover, the worst of both worlds. Pen wasn't sure if this was to his advantage or not. "May we sit down somewhere? I have something I want to show you that I'm hoping you may identify."

This idea was received with amiability. Symo went inside and dragged out a crude bench, its wood silvered with years, to what was obviously its morning warm spot against the wall. The three of them just fit, Pen in the middle. Pen reached into his sash.

Des, get ready to hobble them if they bolt. Try not to hurt them too much.

As you wish.

As he drew out the cloak pin, for a moment he feared exactly that was going to occur, as they both jerked back with guilty recognition. But they settled again, with poorly feigned looks of innocence upon their seamed features.

"Can you tell me where and how you found this?" Pen asked. "It's rather important."

"Never seen it," said skinny Laxo after a moment. His big companion nodded.

Pen sighed. Fair enough. "Well, let me tell you, then. You sold this piece to the proprietress at the clothing shop on Ox Street the day before yesterday. You took it off a newly dead body that you found or stumbled over in an alley somewhere near the Customs house, the prior night. Also his purse. And then his clothes and shoes, because why waste such good cloth on a corpse?" Laxo, it seemed, was wearing Therneas's shoes now, because he tucked his feet discreetly under the bench and looked uncomfortable. "So that brings us back to you two, a bundle of possessions, and a naked body, in the middle of the night in the rain. You could have just walked off then, with no one the wiser."

"Told ya," muttered Laxo across Pen to his companion Symo, who shifted in embarrassment.

"So the question that has been driving me mad for a day is, how did Therneas's body—his name was Therneas, did you know?"

Twin headshakes, truthful this time.

"How did it get into the harbor, and whose nightshirt was he wearing?"

"Uh…mine?" said Symo tentatively.

"*Why?*" Pen was proud that came out of his mouth as not an actual screech.

"Well, we'd got back to the shack, and the clothes were real nice, specially that cloak, made my bed so much warmer, so's it didn't seem fair that we should be warm and he should be left out in the cold all naked. So's I took him back my old nightshirt in trade, because it was the closest I had to a winding sheet. Once we'd got it on him, it looked sort of like the shrouds they bury men in at sea, so we thought maybe it would be more respectful to bury him. You wouldn't want his insulted ghost coming back around, and he'd been generous to us. Couldn't dig a hole in the ground in the middle of town, so's we took him out to the end of the pier instead, slid him over just like off the deck of a ship."

"We said a few words," offered Laxo uneasily.

"Poured a drink in after him, too, just for good fellowship," added Symo. "Laxo thought it was a waste, but I said we shouldn't begrudge."

"How drunk *were* you?"

"Pretty drunk?" said Symo.

"Not as good as the next day, though, after we sold the pin," said Laxo, as if it was a happy memory.

What he can remember of it, said Des dryly.

Or maybe the blotting out of memory was the happy part. Pen was glad he had no duty to judge. Also, it would be unseemly to fold over in helpless laughter at their word-pictures, pained as his guffaws would also be. *Deeply unseemly,* he told his twitching lips, firming them. *God of chaos, did you accept this as a prayer?*

"Well, I can certainly promise you that Therneas's ghost will not be coming back to chide you. Nor anyone else."

Symo brightened. "Gone to his god all right, is he?" He squinted at Pen. "Templeman, would you know?"

"Say rather gone at the hands of his god, and yes."

The pair of them seemed vaguely consoled by this news, offering clumsy tally signs toward their late benefactor. Pen had an urge to sign it backward, signifying erasure, the blotting out of blessing, but they might be shocked.

Symo swallowed in new unease. "You, ah… gonna tell anyone about this, Learned?"

"I have no duty to do so, outside my own Order."

They looked as if they didn't know just how to take this. Also fair enough.

"Looting dead bodies is however a crime, if not one that directly concerns me. Please don't do so again."

"…Shipwreck rules?" offered Laxo.

"No," said Pen firmly. "As you both well know."

The scolded-puppy looks on those old faces were so incongruous, Pen was hard put not to laugh again.

"I should probably examine what of Therneas's clothing and purse remain before I leave you, however. In case there's anything relevant to, um, some other issues."

With great reluctance, they let him inside to do so. The place was tidier than Pen had expected— sailors had to be in the habit of keeping everything firmly secured. The green cloak did make for a warm counterpane upon one of the narrow cots. The rest of the clothes contained no notes or messages, no secret compartments hidden in the seams. The coins left in the small leather purse were anonymous. More handfuls of nothing, and certainly nothing pertinent for the magistrates with respect to Kyem Soudei's case.

Pen kept only the cloak pin, since he'd evidently paid for it.

"There's nothing here I or anyone else can use," he told the pair, handing the possessions back, "and you can. They're yours for all of me. Should any, hm, trailing questions arise from your midnight adventure, you can call on me. Learned Penric, through my chapterhouse. They'll know how to find me."

"Oh," said Symo, surprised and heartened. "That's right nice of you."

"I owe you two something for the information. Don't talk about this otherwise. Truly, don't."

Laxo digested this. After a moment, he thrust out a stoneware jug. "Drink?"

Bastard's teeth not at this hour, Pen suppressed on his lips. He converted it to a politer, "Just a taste. Shall we sit outside?"

Passing the bottle back and forth along the bench, Pen could readily conceal how little of the rotgut wine he actually swallowed. A few leading questions brought out some very good sailor stories from their earlier careers. Time well spent; when he shoved off at last, pleading Temple duties, they waved him away with friendly invitations to return. Which he thought he might take them up on, sometime. Tales, after all, weren't only to be found in books.

He was under no obligation to supply sermons, and hadn't, though he hoped his caution about no-repeat-performances had been taken to heart. *Spiritual advisor* was within his ambit, but however disordered those two's lives were, their souls seemed in rather good shape. Two more interesting new friends in Vilnoc seemed wage enough to Pen for his morning's work. Plus the prize of one more piece of his puzzle put in place.

Pen turned his steps toward the Mother's Order.

PEN ENTERED the hospice courtyard to the sound of raised voices. Clustered around the well were Master Tolga, her shadow Phylos, Alixtra, Captain Oxato, and a man in the garb of a city magistrate, chain of office around his neck, clerk at his elbow. A couple of other soldiers from the ducal guard had evidently given up standing at attention a while ago, and were now sitting on the pavement by the far colonnade passing the time dicing with each other, although with occasional glances at their superior in wait, or hope, of further orders.

"Oh, good, Learned, you're here!" said Alixtra upon spying him, in a tone of relief. All the other faces turned with hers toward Pen, who controlled an urge to back right out again.

He strolled up to the group instead. Oxato gave him his usual perfunctory salute, as a fellow retainer of the duke, and Pen returned his usual perfunctory tally-blessing. Oxato was a sturdy soldier who had lived long enough in Jurgo's service to gain gray hairs and increased responsibilities to give him a few more. Powers that no martial ability, however honed, could defend against tended to put soldiers off their stride, but longer acquaintance had eased him over finding the court sorcerer alarming. Mostly.

Tolga, sounding a little clipped, said, "Please explain to these gentlemen, again, that they are welcome to take the late Master Therneas's body out of here, and I don't care which authority claims custody. I need the cot back for live patients."

"Yes, that's right," said Pen. "By preference the body should be burned, to release the sundered spirit possessing it, and assure no others try to move back in." Had Vissa's body been burned last night, as he'd instructed? Pen hoped that was over with. Trying to feel equally concerned for Therneas's remains was more of a challenge.

"But he hasn't been *tried* yet," said the magistrate in a pressed and rather high-pitched tone.

"Actually, he has," said Pen. "By a higher court than yours. If you want to assure yourself of the state of the husk in there, try finding a heartbeat or a pulse, or take notice that it only draws enough breath to moan." Which Tolga might have done first thing yesterday morning, if she hadn't been so distracted by the corpse's movement, so perhaps the magistrate should be forgiven for his doubt. "Otherwise, I suppose, you can just put it in a cell and wait for its rot to convince you."

Which could be an interesting test, come to think. What Pen had been taught on the subject had not included such post-mortem details. If the body decayed enough, would the sundered ghost depart from it on its own? Would the drain of the occupation speed the ghost's own dissolution, and how long would that take? Had anyone ever recorded such a thing?

Experimental theology, who else would think to invent it? murmured Des. *Only you, Pen.* He ignored the interpolation.

"Our cells are crowded," said the magistrate warily.

"The palace has no dungeon," said Oxato. An evasion; Jurgo used an aging fortress up from the harbor for such legal tasks.

Ah. They hadn't been arguing *for* custody; rather the reverse. Pen wondered if this was anything like the gods debating a sundering from Their side, none wanting to be saddled with a rotting soul.

"Perhaps you could settle this, Learned?" said Alixtra, in a tone of heavy hint. Tolga nodded vigorously.

"How did you come to be here this morning?" Pen asked Alixtra, buying a moment to think. Late morning, by now.

Phylos answered, "Master Tolga sent me to bring you again, Learned, but you weren't home. I thought the acolyte might speak to the matter instead, so I fetched her."

Pen's impulse to say a few sharp things about asking for a Temple advisor and then not listening to her was cut short by Alixtra adding, "Besides, I was wondering how things were getting on."

It was probably not a good idea to bring up what he'd learned from his wharf-rat informants in front of the magistrate, so Pen merely nodded. He could tell her and Tolga later, when they could enjoy it with him.

"Right," Pen sighed. "I rule that Captain Oxato should take charge of the body. Store it in a stall in the palace mews, or in a cell in the fortress, or anywhere you like for now, until you feel it's ready to be burned. That will give time for everyone to resolve all their legal questions. I suppose you'd better gather the ashes, after. You can give the urn to the temple by the hospice to keep, in case any relatives ever turn up to claim them."

Two out of three of the disputants looked pleased at this, a majority rule of sorts.

"But it's *uncanny*," protested Oxato, perhaps in a last-ditch attempt to avoid the responsibility. No, that was unjust; the man was genuinely unnerved.

"Acolyte Alixtra can go with you and your men to deal with any untoward problems, until you have

Therneas's body safely locked up," Pen said. Which, apart from a bit of weakening thrashing and the groans, should be nonexistent. He added quietly aside to Alixtra, "I'll stop by the chapterhouse later and tell you the rest of it." A brief lift of her hand conveyed both acknowledgment and curiosity.

This sop was accepted reluctantly on Oxato's part, and with a touch of aware irony on Alixtra's, but everyone here had other duties waiting. Memory of the scurry after a logjam was broken on a spring river in the Cantons crossed Pen's mind. Tolga lent a stretcher and a couple of dedicats to help the soldiers carry the burden, assuring no more delay. Pen saw the not-quite-funeral procession out. He briefly wondered if the ghost would abandon the body to stay in the hospice where it had died. Evidently not.

He thought he was done for the morning, but the magistrate drew him apart. He was not a man Pen had met before in his varied duties around Vilnoc, which meant that the reverse was also true. He seemed a typical middle-aged functionary, although the fact that he was assigned to this treason-tinged embezzlement case suggested he was experienced. He looked searchingly at Pen;

reassured by his divine's vestments, unsettled by the braids and silver of a sorcerer, averaging to a retreat into professional formality.

"Learned Penric. I understand you were the one who examined Master Therneas's chambers yesterday and found the stolen coin?"

At Pen's nod, he went on, "I need to search them again for any further evidence, although"—he hesitated—"not in the usual way of preparing a case for trial, it seems. Reports will be required, certainly."

"And," Pen suggested gently, "some way of formally clearing the late Kyem Soudei's name from all the false charges he endured?"

The magistrate winced. "That as well."

"Good. I don't think you'll find much there that I didn't, but I'll walk over with you to guide you, if you like."

"Yes, please, Learned," said the magistrate. "I have more than a few questions for you upon what you discovered, and how…"

They started off, trailed by the nervy clerk, ears plainly pricked. The magistrate's questions were mostly shrewd and pertinent. Plainly out of his depth with the theology and magic, he was at least willing to learn to swim.

Pen's answers filled the time it took till the disturbed landlady once more let them into the dead man's lodgings. Pen allowed the magistrate to take over the task of assuring her that no onus fell on her for the behavior of her lodger, though he might be keeping a little suspicion in reserve. If such adjudicators didn't start out untrusting, they tended to become so with wear.

Pen went in with them. He had his own lingering questions, if not the sort the magistrate was addressing. As the man and his clerk gave the place a thorough combing-out, Pen wandered about the chambers, trying to gain some inner sense of Therneas. Most rites of, or prayers for, death magic went unanswered. Why was this one different?

At length, the magistrate concluded that Therneas had concealed nothing here but his hoard, and he and his clerk sat down in the bedroom to make their brief notes. It was the *nothing* that bemused Pen. Had the man ever done more in here but eat, sleep, and count his coin? Though who knew what misadventures he'd engaged in during his earlier crooked-ship-purser days. Which, Pen suspected, had taught him how there might be better, safer pickings ashore, among the very laws he'd evaded. He'd kept no souvenirs of that time. Was there truly no more to the man than his greed? It seemed oddly pure, in a sense.

Fear, Des suggested. *It must have alarmed him to risk a man being put over him as master of the Customs house with the keenness to find his cheating, and immune to being drawn into complicity.*

Yes, hence his cruel destruction of Soudei through his calculated lies. We already knew that. Though it also suggested a few interesting questions to put in the magistrate's ear about the prior master, the one who'd retired. But still not what Pen was seeking.

He sat at Therneas's table, imagining the man sometimes taking out his cases, counting up their contents upon this surface. Could there be some twisted aesthetic aspect, delight in the arts of the mints? But the hoard had hardly been organized as a coin collector would have it. Quantity over quality had seemed the rule.

Pen recalled an old tale of a legendary beast from the Weald, sometimes touched on by bards or nursemaids seeking to thrill their audiences. Ice wyrms lived deep in the mountains, spending their lives in dark caves. There they collected stolen treasure piles, upon which they slept. The monsters could not spend their wealth. They never traded it for any good thing. They just guarded it, endlessly, never daring to leave it, squatting upon it till finally they died of cold and starvation.

So, all right, it was understandable why no god would want such an empty tick of a soul stuck forever to Their side in the impalpable realm beyond death.

As an adult Pen could see the ice wyrm as a cautionary parable against greed, though as a boy, like most boys, it had mostly inspired him to want to search mountain caves. He wasn't sure if he'd have been more delighted by finding the treasure, or the mummified wyrm. Or better, a live one. Any combination would certainly have done.

Or you'd have broken your neck, said Des dryly.

Nearly did, a few times. Never told my mother, of course.

Which brought him back to the other half of his present mystery of death magic. Lack of earthly recourse did seem a condition. Any soul that had made itself ripe for sundering might qualify as an allowed target. The rarity had to lie in the supplicant.

Sincerity must be required, of course. Any inner reservation would be as clear to the white god's eye as sunlight through glass. Who sought death without reservation?

Oh...

It's despair.

Heart destroying. Bone deep down to the marrow. As black as...*a sewer at midnight*, Pen's mind shied from making that a metaphor, but it served. The degree of desolation that would turn a soul not only from life, but the life after. From the held-out hand of any god. A different kind of death by ice. Self-sundering. Soul suicide.

Even the terrible morning Pen had tried to slice through his own arms on that lonely hillside above Martensbridge, he'd only sought death in this world, not beyond. So, not as rock-bottom as he'd thought at the time, eh?

I knew, said Des. *Did you imagine I did not?*

I plead not guilty to that stupidity by reason of insanity. Or vice versa.

Hah. But her inner voice was fond.

Wrath was the more common explanation for spurning the gods, like the outraged ghost from the hospice, so disappointed in what its life had failed to give it that it struck out blindly at any other offer. But despair, too, was counted a deathly sin.

So... Vissa Soudei's answer wasn't justice.
It was grace.

A jolt of a realization, that. Everyone certainly called it justice, *the justice when all other justice fails,* right. Repeated often enough, plainly in casual speech, wrapped up in polysyllables in learned theological discourse. But was it true? Or...entirely true?

Not that it couldn't be both. Parsimony, after all. And a god noted for putting His holy thumb on the scales of events.

Over and over in his career, Pen had confronted the insight that the gods did not care for humans' material concerns, much to the humans' dismay. Only with what record of them was carved into their souls by their unique and individual lives, presented as the final offering upon the altar of their deaths. All deaths, in whatever form. One by one, each attended to with the same singular consideration. Each valuated with the discernment of a connoisseur adding to his collection. Each placed in the niche found most fitting to it. Denied by self-will sometimes, by the gods' will at others, but never lost by *carelessness.*

Duty of care had been the phrase in Pen's training as a divine, parallel and co-equal with his training as a sorcerer. As below, so above? The five purposes of prayer were taught to be service, supplication, gratitude, divination, and atonement, and it was gratitude Penric chose now.

Vissa Soudei was falling through the ice, and You pulled her out.

Thank you, my Lord.

"Are you done here, Learned?" the magistrate's diffident voice asked at his elbow.

"Hm? Oh. Yes. I think I am."

Pen rose and followed the magistrate into the light of the afternoon.

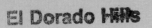

El Dorado Hills